I0614759

Lothair Smith

Smith's Compendium for Stationers and Printers

Lothair Smith

Smith's Compendium for Stationers and Printers

ISBN/EAN: 9783741187483

Manufactured in Europe, USA, Canada, Australia, Japa

Cover: Foto ©Andreas Hilbeck / pixelio.de

Manufactured and distributed by brebook publishing software
(www.brebook.com)

Lothair Smith

Smith's Compendium for Stationers and Printers

SMITH'S

COMPENDIUM

FOR

STATIONERS AND PRINTERS.

COMPILED AND EDITED BY

LOTHAIR SMITH.

ISSUED ANNUALLY.

INDEX.

B

C

PAGE.

3 .

G

H

I

L

M

N

P

R

S

T

LEDGER PAPERS.

Brown's, Weston's, Crane's.

SIZE NAME.	SIZE INCHES.	WEIGHT.	REAM.	100 SHEETS.	QR.
Crown	15 x 19	22	$6.16	$1.29	$0.31
Double Crown.....	19 x 30	44	12.32	2.56	.62
Demy.............	16 x 21	28	8.50	1.77	.43
Demy.............	16 x 21	30	9.50	1.98	.48
Medium...........	18 x 23	36	12.00	2.48	.60
Medium...........	18 x 23	38	13.00	2.69	.65
Medium...........	18 x 23	40	14.00	2.89	.70
Royal.............	19 x 24	44	15.00	3.09	.75
S. Royal	20 x 28	50	20.00	4.13	1.00
Imperial	23 x 31	72	27.00	5.57	1.35
Double Demy......	21 x 32	56	17.00	3.51	.85
Double Demy......	21 x 32	60	19.00	3.92	.95
Double Demy......	16 x 42	56	17.00	3.51	.85
Double Demy......	16 x 42	60	19.00	3.92	.95
Double Medium...	23 x 36	72	24.00	4.95	1.20
Double Medium...	23 x 36	80	28.00	5.78	1.40
Double Medium...	18 x 46	72	24.00	4.95	1.20
Double Medium...	18 x 46	80	28.00	5.78	1.40
Double Royal	24 x 38	88	30.00	6.19	1.50
Double Royal Long	19 x 48	88	30.00	6.19	1.50
Elephant..........	23 x 28	65	27.00	5.75	1.35
Colombier	23 x 34	80	32.00	6.66	1.60
Atlas.............	26 x 33	100	45.00	9.50	2.25
Double Elephant...	27 x 40	125	55.00	12.50	2.75
Antiquarian.......	31 x 53	200	100.00	20.85	5.00
Emperor..........	48 x 72	600	500.00	104.00	25.00

Cap   14 x 17, 14, 16, 18, 20 ⎫
Double Cap 17 x 23. 28, 32, 36, 40 ⎪ 28c. per lb.,
Folio   17 x 22, 20. 22, 24, 28 ⎬ less discount.
Royal Folio 19 x 24, 24, 38 ⎭

Prices subject to discount of 30% full   ream lots.
   "   "   "   20% broken   "   "

Schedule of Prices for Blank-Book Binding Figured on a Basis of 500 Pages, Regular Rulings.

9

PRICE OF BROWN'S, CRANE'S, WESTON'S LINEN LEDGERS. NAME.	$5.04 14x17 18 Cap.	$6.16 15x19 22 Crown.	$8.50 16x21 28 Demy.	$12.00 18x23 36 Med-ium.	$15.00 19x24 44 Royal.	$11.20 17x28 40 Dbl. Cap.	$20.00 20x28 54 S. Royal.	$27.00 23x31 72 Impl.	$17.00 21x32 56 Dbl. Demy.	$24.00 23x36 72 Dbl. Med'm.	$30.00 24x38 88 Dbl. Royal.
Half Roan and Paper	$1.10	$1.20	$1.50	$1.60	$1.90	$1.90	$2.25	$2.75	$2.75	$3.30	$3.70
Half Roan and Cloth	1.20	1.30	1.65	1.75	2.25	2.25	2.60	3.25	3.25	3.75	4.10
Half Russ. and Paper	1.25	1.30	1.50	1.75	2.20	2.60	2.60	3.20	3.20	3.75	4.10
Half Russ. and Cloth	1.40	1.55	1.80	2.20	2.50	2.50	3.00	3.60	3.60	4.40	4.50
Half Russ. and Sheep	1.55	1.75	2.05	2.50	2.95	2.95	3.60	4.50	4.50	5.25	5.25
Spring Back Extra	.25	.30	.50	.50	.65	.65	.65	.90	.90	1.00	1.00
Full Duck Tight Back	1.20	1.30	1.60	1.80	2.25	2.25	2.60	3.25	3.25	3.75	4.00
Full Duck Spring Back	1.80	1.80	2.00	2.50	2.90	2.90	3.20	4.20	4.20	4.60	5.00
Full Roan Tight Back	1.65	1.75	2.00	2.45	3.40	3.40	3.85	4.70	4.75	5.30	5.50
Full Roan Spring Back	2.50	2.60	2.80	3.30	4.50	4.50	5.00	6.00	6.00	6.50	6.75
Full Duck Index	1.00	1.20	1.50	1.70	2.00	2.00	2.25	....	....	....	....
Three-quarter Roan and Paper	1.75	1.85	2.15	2.45	3.25	3.25	3.80	4.75	4.75	5.25	5.50
Three-quarter Roan and Cloth	1.90	2.00	2.35	2.60	3.60	3.60	4.40	5.25	5.25	5.75	6.00
Three-quarter Russ. and Cloth	2.20	2.35	2.85	3.40	4.30	4.30	5.25	6.25	6.25	7.50	7.75
Three-quarter Russ. and Sheep	2.50	2.75	3.30	4.00	5.00	5.00	6.00	7.50	7.50	8.50	9.00
Full Bound Russ. Corners	2.20	2.30	2.50	3.00	3.50	3.60	4.50	5.75	5.75	7.00	7.50
Full Bound Russ. Bands	3.00	3.55	4.25	4.75	5.50	5.50	6.00	8.25	8.25	9.50	10.00
Extra Russ. Bands	4.40	5.30	6.30	7.40	8.50	8.50	9.60	10.70	10.70	11.70	12.25
Full Russ. Plain	5.50	5.30	6.30	7.40	8.50	8.50	9.60	10.70	10.70	11.70	11.70
Full Russ. Ex. Bands	5.75	6.30	7.40	8.50	10.70	10.70	12.60	13.50	13.50	14.75	15.50
Full Russ. Paneled		8.00	8.25	8.75	11.50	11.50	12.50	14.50	14.50	15.50	17.00
Extra 100 Pages	.10	.10	.15	.20	.25	.20	.25	.25	.35	.40	.40
Patent Back Per 100 Pages	.15	.15	.15	.18	.18	.20	.20	.25	.25	.25	.25
Duck Covers	.75	.80	.95	1.10	1.25	1.25	1.50	1.75	1.75	2.00	2.25
Sheep Covers	1.20	1.40	1.65	1.90	2.20	2.20	2.45	3.50	3.50	4.00	4.70
Corners on Covers	.25	.25	.30	.30	.35	.35	.40	.50	.50	.50	.50

Discount to this schedule.

BINDING FLEXIBLE COVERS,

On a Basis of 250-Page Book. Regular Rulings.

STYLE.

Size.	Buffing.	Roan.	Water Grain.	Cow-hide.	Real Russia.
Cap Quarto........	$1.30	$1.40	$1.50	$1.50	$1.75
Demy Quarto....	1.50	1.60	1.75	1.75	2.00
Medium Quarto.	1.75	1.90	2.00	2.00	2.50
Cap......	1.75	1.90	2.00	2.00	2.50
Demy..............	2.25	2.40	2.50	2.50	3.00
Medium...........	2.50	2.60	2.75	2.75	3.50

BINDING CHECKS.

1,000 Checks,	5-deep,	Half Roan and Cloth	.......$1.25
1,000 "	5 "	"	" Paper....... 1.15
500 "	3 "	"	" Cloth .... .80
500 "	3 "	"	" Paper....... .75

Single Check Books, one-third bound, 3 deep, 16c. each.
Single Check Books, one-fourth bound, 3 deep, 8c. each.
Prices on large quantities furnished by estimate.
Loose backs, 25c. extra.
Hinged covers, 25c. extra.
Leather tops and bottoms, 30c. extra.
Side titles, 20c. extra.
Lettering on side each cover, 10c. each.
Numbering and perforating single check books at 20c.
    per 1,000 numbers and 20c. per 1,000 perforations.
Printing names on ends, 25c. per book each impression.
Printing drawer's name on draft, $1 per 1,000.
Printing endorsement on back of checks, $1.20 per 1,000.
Perforating stock checks in quantities:
    10,000 or more at 17c. per 1,000 perforations.
    50,000 "   "   " 15c. "   "   "
    100,000 "   "   " 13c. "   "   "

PRINTING OF BLANK-BOOK HEADINGS.

Crown	15 x 19	} first line of composition, including first token of presswork	$0.75
Cap	14 x 17	} each additional line of composition	.25
Demy	16 x 21	} each additional token of presswork	.25
Folio	17 x 22	}	

Double Cap	17 x 28	} first line of composition, including first token of presswork	$1.00
Medium	18 x 23	} each additional line of composition	.50
Royal	19 x 24	} each additional token of presswork	.50
Super Royal	20 x 28	}	

Double Crown	19 x 30	}	
" Demy	21 x 32	} first line of composition, including first token of presswork	$1.50
" Medium	23 x 36	} each additional line of composition	.75
" Folio	22 x 34	} each additional token of presswork	.75
" Royal	24 x 38	}	
Imperial	23 x 31	}	

Long Double Demy	16 x 42	} first line of composition, including first token of presswork	$2.00
" Medium	18 x 46	} each additional line of composition	1.00
" Royal	19 x 48	} each additional token of presswork	1.00

NOTE.—By token of presswork is meant 250 impressions.

Balance Ledgers..................................$1.00 per column.

11

Prices for Binding of Pamphlets.

Saddle and Side Stitched Wire.

Pages.	Forms.	Number.	Saddle Stitched.	Side Stitched.	
8	1	1,000	$1.30	$1.60	Without Covers.
12	1	"	1.40	1.70	
16	1	"	1.50	1.80	
16	2	"	1.75	2.00	
24	2	"	2.00	2.30	
24	3	"	2.25	2.60	
32	1	"	2.00	2.30	
32	2	"	2.25	2.60	
8	1	"	2.00	3.80	With Covers.
12	1	"	2.20	4.00	
16	1	"	2.20	4.00	
16	2	"	2.50	4.30	
24	2	"	2.75	4.50	
24	3	"	3.00	4.80	
32	1	"	2.50	4.50	
32	2	"	3.00	4.80	
32	3	"		5.00	
32	4	"		5.00	
40	2	"		4.75	
40	3	"		5.00	
40	4	"		5.25	
40	5	"		5.50	
48	2	"		5.00	
48	3	"		5.25	
48	4	"		5.50	
48	5	"		5.75	
48	6	"		6.00	
56	3	"		6.50	
56	4	"		5.75	
56	5	"		6.00	
56	6	"		6.25	
56	7	"		6.50	
64	2	"		5.50	
64	3	"		5.75	
64	4	"		6.00	
64	5	"		6.25	
64	6	"		6.50	
64	7	"		6.75	
64	8	"		7.00	
72	9	"		7.50	

SIZES OF BLANK-BOOK PAGES.

Name.	Length.		Width.
Cap	$13\frac{1}{2}$	x	$8\frac{1}{4}$
Crown	$14\frac{1}{2}$	x	$9\frac{1}{4}$
Demy	$15\frac{1}{2}$	x	$10\frac{1}{4}$
Folio	$16\frac{1}{2}$	x	$10\frac{3}{4}$
Medium	$17\frac{1}{2}$	x	$11\frac{1}{4}$
Royal	$18\frac{1}{2}$	x	$11\frac{3}{4}$
Super Royal	$19\frac{1}{2}$	x	$13\frac{3}{4}$
Imperial	$22\frac{1}{2}$	x	$15\frac{1}{4}$
Double Cap	$16\frac{1}{2}$	x	$13\frac{3}{4}$
" Crown	$18\frac{1}{2}$	x	$14\frac{3}{4}$
" Demy	$20\frac{1}{2}$	x	$15\frac{3}{4}$
" " (long)	$15\frac{1}{2}$	x	$20\frac{3}{4}$
" Medium	$22\frac{1}{2}$	x	$17\frac{3}{4}$
" " (long)	$17\frac{1}{2}$	x	$22\frac{3}{4}$
" Royal	$23\frac{1}{2}$	x	$18\frac{3}{4}$
" " (long)	$18\frac{1}{2}$	x	$23\frac{3}{4}$
Elephant	$22\frac{1}{2}$	x	$13\frac{3}{4}$
Colombier	$22\frac{1}{2}$	x	$16\frac{1}{4}$
Atlas	$25\frac{1}{2}$	x	$16\frac{1}{4}$
Double Elephant	$26\frac{1}{2}$	x	$19\frac{3}{4}$
Antiquarian	$30\frac{1}{2}$	x	$26\frac{1}{4}$

For quarto, divide the length.
For long quarto, divide the width.

Transferring Bonds.

One color.............................$3.00 to $6.00
Two colors............................ 5.00 to 9.00
Three colors.......................... 7.00 to 10.00
Printing bonds, 14 x 17, per 100.................. 2.75
Two colors   "   " 4.00
Three colors   "   " 6.00
Black,   16 x 21, 19 x 24, per 100.............. 3.75
Two colors   "   "   " 6.00
Three colors "   "   " 8.25
Black,   17 x 28, 19 x 30, per 100.............. 4.00
Two colors   "   "   " 7.00
Three colors "   "   " 9.00

Litho Transferring.

Checks, Notes, Drafts, Certificates of Deposit, Re-
  ceipts, Bills of Exchange, Bills of Lading, Policy
  Headings, on 14x17...........................$1.50
Double Transfer, with tinted background, or name
  in outline through body of blank......$2 50 to 3.00
Checks with front and back margin................ 2.00
Eight or ten Blanks to a sheet of flat cap, loose, one
  pattern.. 1.50
Ten Blanks, as above assorted.................... 2.00
Ten or more Blanks to a sheet 19x24 or 17x28, loose,
  one pattern.................................... 2.50
Assorted Patterns................................ 2.50
Checks, 12 on 17x22, 19x24, 17x28, to bind......... 2.25
Letter Heads, 4 on 17x22......................... 1.50
Bill, Note and Statement Headings, 8 on folio...... 1.50

Certificates of Stock, 14x17, 15x19 { one color..... 2.25
                                    { two colors.... 3.75
                                    { three colors.. 5.25

LITHOGRAPHING.

The schedule given below applies to Black Color only. Other colors are from 10 per cent. to 25 per cent. higher, according to color. No schedule for estimating engraving can be given; but, where the order involves a thousand or more impressions, it is safe to assume that the lithographer will reproduce the engraving free, if it is not too elaborate and contains no pictures or vignettes of buildings, etc.

Where an order calls for less than five hundred impressions, figure $1.50 for transfer and $1.50 per hundred impressions.

Transfers of letter, note and bill headings, checks, cards, etc. $1.50.

NUMBER OF IMPRESSIONS.	PRICE.
500	@ 80 cents per 100, transfers extra.
1,000	@ 60 cents per 100, transfers extra.
1,500	@ 60 cents per 100, no transfer.
2,000	@ 55 cents per 100, no transfer.
2,500	@ 50 cents per 100, no transfer.
3,000	@ 50 cents per 100, no transfer.
4,000	@ 40 cents per 100, no transfer.
5,000	@ 35 cents per 100, no transfer.
6,000	@ 30 cents per 100, no transfer.
10,000	@ 28 cents per 100, no transfer.

Bronze should be figured as two printings.

In lithographing checks, as a rule, the orders call for one or two books, and should be figured at $1.50 per 100 impressions, with $1.50 for transfer added.

Lithographing Stock Certificates.

2, on 15 x 19. Two colors, green and black, etc.

250 certificates	$11.62
Black on backs	4.81
500	17.24
Black on backs	7.62
1,000	26.00
Black on backs	12.00
Engraving	$12.00 to 15.00

LITHOGRAPHING BONDS.

Prices include engraving and sketch, good design.
450 words or less in body.

2 colors, 3 printings, 2 on face, 1 on back, 30 or 40 coupons.

Prices exclusive of stock.

250 Bonds............	$70.00
500 "	80.00
1,000 "	95.00
Each additional 100.............	3.00

Prices are based on Lithographers using Stock Borders, Vignettes, etc.

LITHOGRAPHING ENVELOPES.

READY-MADE.

1,000......	$4.00
2,000.............................	6.50
3,000.............................	9.00

Where a larger quantity than 3,000 is ordered it is cheaper to lithograph them flat on sheets. Your envelope manufacturer will make you a lay-out sheet for any size. See Scale " Number cut from a sheet any given size."

LITHOGRAPHED BOND BLANK FORMS.

N. B.—Bond Blanks without Coupons are gotten up WITH or WITHOUT "registration form" lithographed on the back. Please *specify which kind when ordering.* Otherwise, will ship them with registration form lithographed on back.

Quantity.	Registered No. Coupon Blanks.		Lithographed Blanks with 10 or 20 Coupons Attached.		Lithographed Blanks with 40 Coupons Attached.		Lithographed Blanks with 30, 50 or 60 Coupons Attached.	
10	8c	$0.80	14c	$1.40	17c	$1.70	23c	$2.30
25	$6\frac{2}{5}$c	1.60	13c	3.25	16c	4.00	21c	5.25
50	$5\frac{3}{5}$c	2.80	$11\frac{1}{2}$c	5.75	14c	7.00	19c	9.50
75	$5\frac{1}{3}$c	4.00	$10\frac{1}{3}$c	7.75	13c	9.75	17c	12.75
100	$4\frac{4}{5}$c	4.80	9c	9.00	11c	11.00	15c	15.00
150	$4\frac{2}{3}$c	7.00	$8\frac{2}{3}$c	13.00	10c	15.00	14c	21.00
200	$4\frac{1}{2}$c	9.00	$7\frac{1}{2}$c	15.00	9c	18.00	12c	24.00
250	$4\frac{1}{4}$c	10.60	$6\frac{4}{5}$c	17.00	$8\frac{1}{8}$c	20.30	$10\frac{1}{2}$c	26.25
300	4c	12.00	$6\frac{1}{4}$c	18.75	$7\frac{1}{2}$c	22.50	$9\frac{1}{3}$c	28.00
350	$3\frac{11}{16}$c	12.90	$5\frac{5}{7}$c	19.85	$6\frac{5}{7}$c	23.50	$8\frac{3}{7}$c	29.50
400	$3\frac{6}{16}$c	13.50	$5\frac{3}{16}$c	20.75	$6\frac{3}{16}$c	24.75	8c	32.00
450	$3\frac{3}{16}$c	14.30	$4\frac{7}{9}$c	21.50	$5\frac{3}{4}$c	25.90	$7\frac{1}{2}$c	33.75
500	3c	15.00	$4\frac{1}{2}$c	22.50	$5\frac{2}{5}$c	27.00	$7\frac{1}{5}$c	36.00
1,000	$2\frac{7}{10}$c	27.00	4c	40.00	$4\frac{4}{5}$c	48.00	$6\frac{1}{4}$c	62.50

Above prices net by F. R. WARLEY, 180 Broadway, N. Y.

STOCK CERTIFICATES COMPLETE.

Printed, Numbered and Bound.

	Cheaper Style.	Best Style.		Cheaper Style.	Best Style.
50	$3.00	$4.50	350	$9.00	$10.50
100	4.00	5.50	400	10.00	11.50
150	5.00	6.50	450	11.00	12.50
200	6.00	7.50	500	12.00	13.50
250	7.00	8.50	1,000	23.00	25.00
300	8.00	9.50			

Certificates designated by letters are sold only in the better and higher-priced form; those larger than 14 x 8½ are charged at $1 per hundred extra. The price for 1,000 includes binding in two books.

These prices are for the usual form of stock certificates. Extra for printing name on back, 75c. to $1. Prices for special forms on application.

Above prices subject to a discount of 20 and 5.

Prices by courtesy of A. B. King & Co., 105 William Street, New York.

STOCK CERTIFICATE BLANKS.

1 to 60 certificate blanks (not gold certificates).. 1½ cents each.
61 to 100   "   "   ("   "   ).. $1.00
In quantities over 100 .... 1 cent each.

GOLD CERTIFICATE BLANKS.

Special Prices.

1 to 70 gold certificate blanks (not regular goods)... 2 cents each.
71 to 100   "   "   ("   "   )... $1.50
Gold certificates, in quantities over 100............... 1⅛ cents each.

Above prices net.

By courtesy of F. R. Warley, 180 Broadway. Telephone, 4383 Cortlandt.

A. B. KING'S BONDS COMPLETE.

Printed and Numbered.

	Without Coupons.	10 Coupons.	20 Coupons.	30 Coupons.	40 Coupons.	50 Coupons.	60 Coupons.
25	$14.00	$24.00	$29.00	$34.00	$39.00	$43.00	$46.00
50	16.00	26.00	31.00	36.00	41.00	46.00	49.00
75	18.00	28.00	33.00	38.00	43.00	48.00	52.00
100	20.00	30.00	35.00	40.00	45.00	50.00	55.00
200	27.00	37.00	43.00	49.00	55.00	61.00	67.00
300	34.00	44.00	51.00	58.00	65.00	72.00	79.00
400	41.00	51.00	59.00	67.00	75.00	83.00	91.00
500	48.00	58.00	67.00	76.00	85.00	94.00	103.00

Our newest designs are elegantly lithographed on Crane's No. 21 Bond.

Above prices subject to a discount of 20 and 5 per cent.

Printing of Note, Letter and Bill Heads, Receipts, Order Blanks and Small Blanks, Note Circulars, Hand Bills, Cards, Etc.

	Black Ink.
1,000	$0.75
2,000	1.25
3,000	1.80
5,000	2.50
10,000	4.50

For colored ink, add 10 cents per 1,000 impressions.

Where composition is very elaborate it will be charged at the rate of 50 cents per hour.

Bookwork: No scale can be given for bookwork, as it depends upon matter, face of type, number of cuts, etc.

Hand composition is as a rule figured at from 50 to 75 cents per 1,000 ems, and double rate for tabular work.

Linotype composition is figured from 25 to 40 cents per 1,000 ems, according to matter, and cannot be set in one slug wider than 25 ems pica. Most good printers do not advocate linotype composition for fine bookwork.

DATING.

Dating Bank Ticklers.

Printing one year, without days	$3.00
Printing two years, without days	4.00
Printing three years, without days	5.00
Printing four years, without days	6.00
Printing five years, without days	7.00
Printing one year, with days	4.00
Printing two years, with days	7.00
Printing three years, with days	9.00
Printing four years, with days	11.00
Printing five years, with days	13.00

TRADE PRICE LIST PRINTING.

Posters and Show Cards, Including Stock.

Extra-Mammoth—33 x 46.

	White Paper.	Ass'td Paper.	Col'd Ink.	In Two Colors.
One Hundred......	$4.50	....	$6.00	$8.00
Two "	6.75	....	8.25	11.50
Three "	8.50	....	10.50	15.00
Five "	11.00	....	13.50	21.50
One Thousand	17.00	....	21.00	30.00

Mammoth—28 x 42.

	White Paper.	Ass'td Paper.	Col'd Ink.	In Two Colors.
Fifty...............	....	$2.75	....	....
One Hundred......	$3.00	3.25	$4.25	$6.50
Two "	4.50	5.00	6.25	9.00
Three "	5 75	6.25	7.50	11.00
Five "	8.00	8.75	10.00	15.00
One Thousand.....	12.50	13.50	15.25	23.75

Double-Medium—24 x 38.

	White Paper.	Ass'td Paper.	Col'd Ink.	In Two Colors.
Fifty...............	....	$2.50	....	....
One Hundred......	$2.75	3.00	$4.00	$6.00
Two "	4.00	4.25	5.50	8.50
Three "	5.00	5.50	6.75	10.25
Five "	7.00	7.75	9.00	14.00
One Thousand.....	10.50	11.50	13.25	31.75

Half-Mammoth—21 x 28.

	White Paper.	Ass'td Paper.	Col'd Ink.	In Two Colors.
Fifty...............	....	$2.25	....	....
One Hundred......	$2.50	2.75	$3.50	$5.00
Two "	3.25	3.75	4.50	6.50
Three "	4.00	4.75	5.50	8.00
Five "	5.50	6.00	7.25	10.00
One Thousand.....	7.50	8.50	10.00	13.00

Medium—19 x 24.

	White Paper.	Ass'td Paper.	Col'd Ink.	In Two Colors.
Fifty...............	....	$2.00	....	....
One Hundred......	$2.25	2.50	$3.25	$4.75
Two "	2.75	3.00	4.00	6.00
Three "	3.25	3.75	4.75	6.75
Five "	4.25	4.75	6.25	9.00
One Thousand.....	6.50	7.00	9.00	12.00

Half-Medium—12 x 19.

	White Paper.	Ass'td Paper.	Col'd Ink.	In Two Colors.
Fifty...............	....	$1.50	....	....
One Hundred......	$1.75	2.00	$3.00	$4.00
Two "	2.25	2.50	3.75	5.00
Three "	2.75	3.00	4.50	6.00
Five "	3.50	3.75	5.50	7.25
One Thousand.....	4.50	5.00	6.75	10.00

Curbstone—8 x 19.

	WHITE PAPER.	ASS'TD PAPER.	COL'D INK.	IN TWO COLORS.
Five Hundred......	$2.00	$2.50	$3.00	$4.00
One Thousand	2.75	3.25	3.50	5.00
Two "	4.00	4.75	6.75	9.00
Five "	9.00	11.00	13.00	19.00
Ten "	16.00	19.00	24.00	35.00

Show Cards—11 x 11 or 11 x 14.

Fifty..............	$2.25	....	$3.00	$4.50
One Hundred......	2.75	....	3.75	5.00
Two "	4.00	....	5.00	7.00
Three "	5.25	....	6.00	9.00

14 x 14 or 14 x 22.

Fifty..............	$3.00	....	$3.50	$5.00
One Hundred......	4.00	....	4.75	6.00
Two "	6.00	....	7.50	8.50
Three "	8.00	....	9.50	11.00

No extra charge for Borders or Stock Cuts. We have cuts of the Official Emblems of all the Political Parties. Heavy composition charged extra, according to time taken.

TERMS.—A discount of 15% for cash.

Theatrical Hangers.

14 x 42 or 21 x 28, one hundred, black ink........	$3.00
Each additional hundred.........................	0.50
12 x 38 or 19 x 24, one hundred, black ink..	2.75
Each additional hundred.........................	0.50

Prices by courtesy JOHN L. CAMERON,
57 Ann Street., N. Y.

Indexing Blank Books.

Plain Indexing......................25 cents per book.	
Extension Leather Tabs..............50 " "	
Index in front......................20 " "	

Lettering Blank Books.

Black or Gold, Back.................. 5 cents per line.	
Side lettering......................10 " "	
Leather side title ....10 " extra.	

Imprinting Revenue Stamps on Checks, Notes, Drafts, Etc.

Under the Government regulations which went into effect July 1st, the prices for imprinting are uniform with all contractors and inflexible, viz. : 80 cents per thousand stamps imprinted, when imprinted upon sheets containing five or more stamps, and $1 per thousand stamps when imprinted upon sheets containing less than five stamps to the sheet, and all freight or delivery charges must be paid by the parties ordering.

Note.—You pay contractor for imprinting only, as contractors for imprinting are forbidden to receive remittances for stamps. The payment for stamps must accompany your request to the collector for the requisition. This new ruling is to be rigidly enforced.

Your request for requisitions must be made on your firm letter head, stating number of stamps, amount in dollars and cents, and contractor who is to do the imprinting.

Allow as much time as possible, as it is a difficult matter to hurry through a requisition. There are others; remember that.

Collector for New York City: American Tract Society Building, Nassau and Spruce Street, New York.

BLACK BORDERING

ON

Note Paper} 5 quire lots, 10 cents per quire.
Envelopes } Ream lots, $1.50 per ream.
Visiting } Cards, 15 cents per pack.
Memorial} $1.50 per 1,000 cards.

Borders of white, red, blue, etc., can be put on at above prices.

H. A. McAfee & Son, 21 Beekman St., New York.

ELECTROTYPING.

Job Work blocked on wood, 2 cents per square inch; minimum charge, 12 cents.

Blocked on solid or cored metal, 6 cents per square inch; minimum charge, 24 cents.

Job Work not blocked, 10 per cent. less than scale price; minimum charge, 12 cents.

Half-Tone Electrotypes blocked on wood, 3 cents per square inch; minimum charge, 18 cents.

Blocked on solid or cored metal, 7 cents per square inch; minimum charge, 36 cents.

Not blocked, 10 per cent. less than scale; minimum charge, 18 cents.

Blocking Job or Bookwork Plates on wood, 10 cents each; two or more plates, 7 cents each. Larger than 15 square inches, ½ cent per square inch; minimum charge, 12 cents.

Blocking on solid or cored metal, 4 cents per square inch; minimum charge, 25 cents. Two or more, 20 cents each.

Catalogue Work, same price.

Bookwork not blocked, 1¼ cent per square inch; minimum, 15 cents per page—16 pages to be a book; less than 16 pages at the rate of 1½ cents per square inch; minimum charge, 15 cents.

Stereotype Job Work, 15 per cent. less than above scale; minimum, 12 cents.

Stereotype Book Work, not blocked, 1 cent per square inch; minimum, 12 cents.

Electrotype Shells, half-scale price.

Time, 70 cents per hour.

Backing up Half-Tone Plates, 2 cents per square incn; minimum, 25 cents. Two or more, 20 cents each.

Binders' Stamps, double-scale price; minimum, 24 cents.

Engravers' Metal, 18 x 24 or over, at 20 cents per pound.

Paneled Blocks containing over 50 square inches, ¾ cents per square inch; under 50 inches, 1 cent per square inch; minimum, 40 cents.

Plain Morticing in Wood, 12 cents; Metal, 24 cents.

Notching Wood, 6 cents; Metal, 12 cents.

COPPER PLATE ENGRAVING.

VISITING.

Engraving Name, Script (name only)............. $0.40
Engraving Name, Script (Mr. and Mrs.)........... 50
Engraving Name, Roman....................... 1.25
Engraving Name, Gothic....................... 1.00
Engraving Name, Old English, cross-shaded....... 1.50
Engraving Name, Old English, solid.............. 1.00
Engraving Name, Facsimile..................... 1.00
Engraving Address or Day, Script................ 20
Engraving Address or Day, Roman............... 1.00
Engraving Address or Day, Gothic............... 75

WEDDING.

Engraving Wedding Plates, per line.............. $.50
Engraving Reception Plates, per line............. 40
Engraving At Home Plates, per line.............. 40
Engraving Church Plates, per line............... 40
Engraving Wedding Monogram on Plate, Script.... 1.00
Engraving Wedding Monogram on Plate, Orna-
mental 2.00
Engraving School Commencements, per line....... 60

BUSINESS CARDS.

Engraving Firm Name, Heavy Script.............. $0.75
Engraving Firm Name, Medium Heavy Script..... 50
Engraving Firm Name, Roman................... 1.25
Engraving Firm Name, Old English.......$1.00 to 1.50
Engraving each additional line, Script, according to
size .... 25c. to 35
Engraving each additional line, Roman, according
to size.............................$1.00 to 1.25
Engraving each additional line, Gothic, according
to size.............................75c. to 1.00

STEEL DIE ENGRAVING.

ADDRESSES.

Engraving 1 line, Gothic.......................... $1.00
Engraving 1 line, Old English...... .... 1.00
Engraving 1 line, Roman........................ 1.25
Engraving 2 lines, above, according to size,
                                        $1.75 to 2.00
Fancy or ornamental lines charged extra.

MONOGRAMS.

Engraving Monogram, Script.................... $1.00
Engraving Monogram, cross-shaded letters......... 1.25
Engraving Monogram, sunk...............$2.00 to 2.50
Engraving Monogram, Circle and Ribbon....1.75 to 2.50
Engraving Monogram, Facsimile............1.00 to 1.50

COMMERCIAL.

Engraving Die, 1 x 3 inches, first line.............. $1.25
Engraving second line.......... .... 1.00
Engraving third line............................. 75
Engraving fourth line and after, per line............ 50

Larger dies than above will be charged extra, according to amount of work.

PHOTO ENGRAVING, ETC.

Half Tone, 15c. to 25c. per sq. inch, minimum charge.......... $2.00
Line,   8c.   "   "   "   "   60

PLATE PRINTING.

VISITING.

Printing 100 Visiting Cards........................ $0.40
Printing 50 Visiting Cards....................... 20

WEDDINGS, ETC.

Printing 100 Wedding Invitations................. $1.00
Printing 100 Wedding Invitations, Gold or Silver... 1.50
Printing 100 Reception Cards.................... 60
Printing 100 At Home Cards 60
Printing 100 Church Cards...................... 50
Printing 100 Wedding Envelopes............. 60

NOTE.—Above in quantities of 1,000 or more at reduced rates.

COMMERCIAL.

Printing 1,000 small Business Cards............... $4.50
Printing 1,000 large Business Cards.............. 5.00
Printing 1,000 Note Heads...................... 5.00
Printing 1,000 Letter Heads.............. $5.00 to 6.00
Printing 1,000 Statements................ 5.00 to 6.00
Printing 1,000 Business Envelopes .... 4.50 to 5.00
Printing 1,000 Professional Statements............ 8.00

STEEL DIE EMBOSSING.

Monogram or Address Dies, any colors, per quire
or pack $0.06
Stamping, Bronze, Burnished, per quire or pack,
according to the size of die.............12c. to   15
Stamping, no color, per quire or pack............   05
    "   500 Single Sheets, any colors.......... 1.00
    "   500 Folded Sheets, any colors.......... 1.20
    "   1,000 Single Sheets........ .... 1.75
    "   1,000 Folded Sheets.................... 2.00
    "   1,000 Bronze......................... 4.00
    "   1,000 Bronze and Burnished............ 4.50
    "   1,000 Plain, no color, small dies........   50

ILLUMINATING.

Two Colors, per quire or pack..............30c. to   40
Three Colors, per quire or pack...........40c. to   50

These prices vary according to size of die.

Sectional Dies stamped in colors, flags, crests, coats-of-arms, etc., at 20c. per quire for each color.

ANY COLOR INK.

Prices per 1,000 impressions.

Quantity.	Single Sheets.	Envelopes.	Folded Sheets.
1,000 to 3,000 imp..........	$1.50......	$1.50......	$1.75
5,000 imp..................	1.40......	1.40......	1.50
10,000 imp.................	1.30......	1.25......	1.40
20,000 or more imp..........	1.20......	1.10......	1.30

Plain embossing (no color), in quantities, special prices will be quoted upon application.

NOTE.—The above prices are for dies 1 x 3 inches or smaller. Extra charges for larger or special die work.

CARD STOCK.

VISITING AND RECEPTION.
Plate or Kid Finish.

100 Cards, Ivory	$0.30
100 Cards, 2 or 3 ply Wedding Bristol	25
50 Cards, 2 or 3 ply Wedding Bristol...........	15
100 Reception Cards............................	40
100 At Home Cards.............................	40
100 Church Cards..............................	25
500 Cards	1.00
1,000 Cards	1.75

MOURNING CARDS.
See Schedule " Black Bordering."

CARD ENVELOPES.

100 Envelopes to fit any size card..................	$0.35
100 Envelopes, Black Bordered..............	75

WEDDING STOCK.

100 Sets, $3\frac{1}{2}$ size, 80 lb., plate or kid finish........	$1.50
100 Sets, $4\frac{1}{2}$ size, 80 lb., plate or kid finish.........	2.00
100 Sets, $7\frac{1}{5}$ size, 80 lb., plate or kid finish.........	2.00
100 Sets, Consuelo size, 80 lb., plate or kid finish...	2.00

SIZES OF WEDDINGS IN INCHES.

71-5 measures (folded)........................	$6\frac{7}{16}$ x $4\frac{13}{16}$
81-3½ " "	$6\frac{3}{8}$ x $4\frac{1}{4}$
81-4½ " "	$6\frac{7}{8}$ x $4\frac{7}{16}$
81-5½ " "	$6\frac{5}{16}$ x $5\frac{5}{8}$
81-6 " "	$7\frac{7}{8}$ x $4\frac{7}{8}$
Consuelo measures (folded)...................	$6\frac{1}{2}$ x $5\frac{13}{16}$

Whiting's sizes.

Prices for Ruling Note, Letter, Bill Heads and Statements.

SIZE OF PAPER.	NUMBER REAMS.	NOTE OR LETTER. One Side.	NOTE OR LETTER. Two Sides.	BILLS. One Side.	STATEMENTS. Two Sides.
Cap 14 x 17........	1	....	....	$0.65	$0 90
" " "	2	....	....	1.20	1.80
" " "	5	..	....	2.25	3.75
" " "	10	....	....	4.00	6.00
Demy, Folio Royal	1	$0.50	$0.60	. .	....
	2	1.00	1.20	....	....
	5	2.25	2.50	....	....
	10	4.00	5.00	....	. ..
Single 1,000 Headings	..	....	.30	....	....

Prices for Ruling Blanks, Demy or Smaller, Not Exceeding 20 Down Pens.

	100	250	500	1,000	ADDED 100
1 Run........	$0.85	$0.95	$1.00	$1.30	$0.05
2 Runs.......	1.40	1.60	1.90	2.40	.08
3 Runs.......	1.90	2.15	2.60	3.15	.12
4 Runs.......	2.40	2.70	3.20	3.90	.15

DOUBLE CAP (17 X 28) OR SMALLER, NOT EXCEEDING 40 DOWN PENS.

	100	250	500	1,000	ADDED 100
1 Run........	$0.90	$1.15	$1.55	$1.90	$0.06
2 Runs.......	1.70	2.00	2.40	3.00	.12
3 Runs..	2.40	2.75	3.40	4.15	.15
4 Runs.......	2.90	3.40	4.00	4.90	.18

DOUBLE DEMY (21 X 32) OR SMALLER, NOT EXCEEDING 60 DOWN PENS.

	100	250	500	1,000	ADDED 100
1 Run........	$1.40	$1.90	$2.65	$3.15	$0.08
2 Runs.........	2.15	2.65	3.40	4 15	.16
3 Runs.......	2.90	3.40	4.15	5.15	.20
4 Runs.......	3.65	4.65	4.90	6.15	.25

DOUBLE MEDIUM (23 X 36) OR SMALLER, NOT EXCEEDING 80 DOWN PENS.

	100	250	500	1,000	ADDED 100
1 Run........	$1.90	$2.40	$2.90	$3.65	$0.10
2 Runs..... .	2.90	3.40	3.90	4.90	.20
3 Runs	3.90	4.40	4.90	6.15	.25
4 Runs	4.90	5.40	5.90	7.40	.30

It is quite impossible to make a table of prices covering all blanks. This is given as a guide, but should only be used as an approximate price.

RULED STOCK,

FROM BASIS OF PAPER COSTING, PLAIN, 12, 10 AND 8 CENTS.

		Price per 1,000. 12c.	10c.	8c.
Bill Heads, 14-lb. 6s		$0.66	$0.54	$0.42
" 14-lb. 4s		98	81	63
" 14-lb. 2s		1.96		
" 16-lb. 6s		75	62	48
" 16-lb. 4s		1.12	92	72
" 16-lb. ⅔s		1.50		
" 16-lb. 2s		2.24	1.84	1.44
" 18-lb. 6s		84		
" 18-lb. 4s		1.26		
" 18-lb. 2s		2.52		
" Narrow Cut, 16-lb. 6s		75		
" " 16-lb. 4s		1.12		
" " 16-lb. 2s		2.24		
Note Heads, 6-lb. Demy	Ruled one or both sides.	84		
" 5-lb. Folio		70	58	
" 6-lb. Folio		84	69	54
" 6-lb. Packet		84		
" 7-lb. Packet		98	81	63
" 8-lb. Packet		1.12		
" 7-lb. Royal		98		
" 8-lb. Royal		1.12		
Letter Heads, 10-lb. Demy		1.40		
" 12-lb. Demy		1.68	1.38	1 08
" 12-lb. Folio		1.68		
Statements, 6-lb. Demy		84		
" 5-lb. Folio		70	58	
" ⅔, 5-lb. Folio		47		
" 6-lb. Folio		84	69	54
" ⅔, 6-lb. Folio		56	46	
" 11-inch, 8-lb. Folio		1.12		
" 17-inch, 12-lb. Folio		1.68		
" 16-lb. Cap		75	62	48
" ⅔, 16-lb. Cap		50	42	32
" dollars and cents, 16-lb. Cap		75		
" 11-inch, 16-lb. Cap		1.00		
" 17-inch, 16-lb. Long Cap		1.50		
" 20-lb. Folio, Medium	Single or Double.	47	39	27
" 20-lb. Folio, Long Med.		70		
" 20-lb. Folio, Infants		32	26	18
" 20-lb. Folio, Obl. Infts.		47	39	27

Colored Bill Heads, 16-lb. 6s	$0.80
" " 16-lb. 4s	1.20
" " 16-lb. 2s	2.40
" Statements, 6-lb	96
" Note Heads, 6-lb	96

CREAM LAID, CARMINE RULED.

Letter Heads, 12-lb.	$1.80
Packet Note Heads, 7-lb	1.05
Envelopes to match	1.25

POSTERS AND HAND BILLS.

No.	Size. Per 1,000.	Straw.	Rag.	Col. News.	Book.
16s,	6 x 9	$0.12	$0.24	$0.20	$0.35
21s,	5 x 8	12	24	20	35
24s,	4½ x 8	10	20	14	24
32s,	4½ x 6	7	14	10	17
12s,	6 x 12	17	34	28	48
8s,	9 x 12	24	48	40	70

188 MR. ROBERT GURNEY HAVEN.

189 MRS. EDMUND CLINTON JOHNSTON.

190 MR. JOHN RAE LAURENCE.

191 MRS. NICHOLAS A. GREENE.

192 Mr. Charles Gordon Phillips.

193 Mrs. Herbert A. Russell.

H. G. A. & CO.

S 1

S 2

S 3

S 5

S 6

S 7

S 8

IN MAKING BLANK BOOK PATTERNS SPECIFY THE ABOVE
NUMBERS. ALL BINDERS WILL HAVE A COPY.

Styles of Engraving.

168 . Mr. William W. Astor.

169 . Mr. John W. Beekman.

170 _ Mrs. James _ Sloan.

171 . Mrs. Herbert Alexandre.

172 . Mr. Russell B. Hoyt.

173 _ Miss Whitman _

174: . Mr. Henry Lewis

THE VERY LATEST SIZES AND FINEST CARD BOARD USED.
ORDER BY NUMBER.

H. G. ALFORD & CO.

ENGRAVERS, PRINTERS & EMBOSSERS

TO THE TRADE

96 - 98 FULTON ST., NEW YORK.

PRICE LIST OF No. 1 RAG ENVELOPES.

	COMMERCIAL SIZES.							OFFICIAL SIZES—All High Cut.						
SIZE NUMBER......	2—3	4	5	5½	6	6½	6¾	7	8½	9	10	11	12	14
SIZE IN INCHES.....	2-$2\frac{5}{8}$x$4\frac{1}{4}$ 3-$2\frac{5}{8}$x$4\frac{11}{16}$	$2\frac{7}{8}$x$5\frac{3}{16}$	$3\frac{1}{8}$x$5\frac{7}{16}$	$3\frac{3}{16}$x$5\frac{1}{2}$	$3\frac{9}{16}$x6	$3\frac{5}{8}$x$6\frac{1}{4}$	$3\frac{5}{8}$x$6\frac{1}{2}$	$3\frac{3}{4}$x$6\frac{3}{4}$	$3\frac{7}{8}$x$8\frac{1}{4}$	4x$9\frac{1}{16}$	$4\frac{1}{8}$x$9\frac{1}{2}$	$4\frac{7}{16}$x$10\frac{5}{16}$	$4\frac{5}{8}$x$11\frac{1}{8}$	$4\frac{3}{4}$x$11\frac{1}{2}$
40-lb. No. 1 Gov......		$0.64	$0.67	....	$0.83	$0.85	$0.90							
High Cut.........	$0.60	.66	.70	.80	.85	.90	.95	$1.05	$1.20	$1.32	$1.37	$1.72	$1.90	$2.00
50-lb. No. 1 Gov....		.75	.81	...	.98	1.00	1.05							
High Cut..........	.72	.80	.85	.95	1.00	1.05	1.10	1.23	1.44	1.57	1.62	2.12	2.32	2.62
60-lb. No. 1 Gov. ..		.86	.94	....	1.12	1.17	1.25							
High Cut..........	.80	.89	.98	1.10	1.17	1.25	1.30	1.44	1.67	1.84	1.95	2.42	2.75	2.97

BARONIALS.

SIZE NUMBER....................................	3	4	5	6	7
SIZE IN INCHES....................................	$3\frac{5}{16}$x4	$3\frac{11}{16}$x$4\frac{3}{4}$	4x$5\frac{1}{8}$	$4\frac{1}{2}$x$5\frac{1}{2}$	$4\frac{1}{2}$x$5\frac{3}{4}$
50-lb. No. 1....................................	$0.85	$0.90	$1.05	$1.65	$1.75
60-lb. No. 1....................................	.95	1.00	1.20	1.85	1.95

CLOTH LINED, WHITE OR BLUE. 100 Box.

SIZE NUMBER................	7	8½	9	10	11	12	13	14	15
SIZE IN INCHES................	$3\frac{3}{4}$x$6\frac{3}{4}$	$3\frac{3}{4}$x$8\frac{1}{4}$	4x$4\frac{1}{16}$	$4\frac{1}{8}$x$9\frac{1}{2}$	$4\frac{7}{16}$x$10\frac{5}{16}$	$4\frac{5}{8}$x$11\frac{1}{8}$	5x11	$4\frac{3}{4}$x$11\frac{1}{2}$	5x12
White or Blue................	$11.00	$12.00	$13.00	$14.00	$16.00	$18.50	$20.50	$20.50	$23.00

DENNISON'S CLASP ENVELOPE.

OPEN END, PURE JUTE MANILA, XXXX WEIGHT.

No.	Size.	Price per M.	No.	Size.	Price per M.	No.	Size.	Price per M.	No.	Size.	Price per M.	No.	Size.	Price per M.	No.	Size.	Price per M.
0	$2\frac{1}{2}$x$4\frac{1}{4}$	$4.00	20	$3\frac{7}{8}$x$7\frac{1}{2}$	$4 75	40	$5\frac{3}{8}$x$7\frac{1}{2}$	$5 50	55	6 x 9	$6 25	70	7 x$10\frac{1}{2}$	$8.00	11	$4\frac{3}{8}$ x$10\frac{1}{4}$	$6.90
5	$3\frac{1}{8}$x$5\frac{1}{2}$	4.25	25	$4\frac{5}{8}$x$6\frac{3}{4}$	5.00	45	$5\frac{1}{4}$x8	5.75	60	$6\frac{1}{4}$x $9\frac{1}{2}$	6.75	9	4 x 9	6.10	12	$4\frac{5}{8}$ x$10\frac{5}{8}$	7.20
10	$3\frac{3}{8}$x6	4.50	30	$4\frac{7}{8}$x$7\frac{1}{4}$	5 00	50	$5\frac{1}{2}$x$8\frac{1}{4}$	6.00	65	$6\frac{1}{2}$x10	7.50	9½	$4\frac{1}{8}$x$9\frac{5}{8}$	6.25	14	$4\frac{13}{16}$x$11\frac{1}{2}$	7.80
15	4 x$6\frac{3}{8}$	4.75	35	5 x$7\frac{1}{2}$	5.25												

Prices for printing: 1,000, 75c.; 3,000 @ 60c., 5,000 @ 45c. per M.

Discount 20% on Clasp Envelopes.

DENNISON MFG. CO.,
BOSTON, NEW YORK, PHILADELPHIA, CHICAGO, CINCINNATI and ST. LOUIS.

OBLONG AND SQUARE ENVELOPES.

XX MANILA AND XX WHITE.

2 Series, 31 Sizes, in Stock, put up 500 in Box.

OBLONG SERIES.

No.		Long.		Wide.	XX WHITE. Per 1,000.	XX WHITE. Per 100.	XX MANILA. Per 1,000.	XX MANILA. Per 100.
1	C. C.	3⅝	x	5½	$1.75	$0.20	$1.25	$0.15
2	"	4¼	x	6⅛	1.90	.20	1.30	.15
3	"	4⅜	x	6½	1.55	.20	1.30	.20
4	"	4⅜	x	7¼	1.75	.20	1.40	.20
5	"	4¾	x	7⅛	2.00	.25	1.95	.25
6	"	5¼	x	7⅞	2.25	.25	1.95	.25
7	"	5⅜	x	8½	2.25	.25	2.00	.25
8	"	5⅜	x	9½	2.50	.30	2.00	.25
9	"	5⅝	x	9¼	2.50	.30	2.00	.25
10	"	6¼	x	9¼	3.00	.40	2.50	.30
11	"	6½	x	10	3.25	.40	2.50	.30
12	"	5	x	7⅞	2.25	.25	2.00	.25
13	"	6½	x	9½	3.25	.40	3.00	.40

20 SIZES, put up assorted (500), in box.
XX White, $3.50 per M. net.
XX Manila, $2.50 per M. net.

SQUARE SERIES.

No.		Long.		Wide.	XX WHITE. Per 1,000.	XX WHITE. Per 100.	XX MANILA. Per 1,000.	XX MANILA. Per 100.
20	C. C.	3⅝	x	4⅝	$0.75	$0.15	$0.65	$0.10
21	"	4⅛	x	5⅛	.85	.15	.75	.10
22	"	4¼	x	5⅜	1.25	.20	1.15	.15
23	"	4⅛	x	6	1.25	.20	1.15	.15
24	"	4½	x	5¾	1.50	.20	1.25	.20
25	"	4⅞	x	6	1.55	.20	1.30	.20
26	"	5	x	6½	1.75	.25	1.40	.20
27	"	5½	x	7¼	2.45	.30	2.00	.25
28	"	5⅜	x	7½	2.65	.30	2.25	.30
29	"	7	x	8¼	3.30	.40	2.50	.30
30	"	6¾	x	9	3.75	.45	2.75	.30
31	"	7⅛	x	9¼	3.90	.50	3.00	.35
32	"	8½	x	10½	6.50	.75	4.50	.50
33	"	9	x	11½	6.50	.75	4.50	.50
34	"	6	x	6	2.45	.35	2.00	.25
35	"	4⅝	x	6¾	2.35	.25	2.00	.25
36	"	5⅜	x	6¾	2.45	.25	2.20	.25
37	"	5⅛	x	6⅞	2.50	.25	2.25	.25

GOVERNMENT ENVELOPES.

Post-Office Department Schedule of January 1, 1899.

DESIGNATION, QUALITY DENOMINATION AND DIMENSIONS.	COLOR.	1,000	500
No. 1-1st....2-cent....2⅞ x 5¼ inches	White only	$21.12	$10.56
No. 2-1st....1-cent....3¼ x 5½ "	White or amber	11.20	5.60
No. 2-1st... 2-cent.... " "	White or amber	21.20	10.60
No. 2-2d.....2-cent.... " "	Buff or blue	21.00	10.50
No. 3-1st....1-cent....3⅜ x 5⅞ "	White or amber	11.20	5.60
No. 3-1st....2-cent.... " "	White or amber	21.20	10.60
No. 3-2d.....2-cent.... " "	Buff or blue	21.00	10.50
No. 3-1st....5 cent.... " "	White or amber	51.20	25.60
No. 4-1st....2-cent....3⅝ x 5⅞ "	White or amber	21.20	10.60
No. 5-1st....1-cent....3½ x $6\frac{5}{16}$ "	White or amber	11.20	5.60
No. 5-1st... 2-cent.... " "	White or amber	21.20	10.60
No. 5-2d.....2-cent.... " "	Buff or blue	21.08	10.54
No. 5-1st....5-cent.... " "	White or amber	51.20	25.60
No. 7-1st....2-cent....3⅞ x 8⅞ "	White or amber	21.80	10.90
No. 7-2d.....2-cent.... " "	Buff or blue	21.40	10.70
No. 7-1st....4-cent.... " "	White or amber	41.80	20.90
No. 8-1st....2-cent....4⅛ x 9½ "	White or amber	21.80	10.90
No. 8-1st....4-cent.... " "	White or amber	41.80	20.90
No. 9-1st....2-cent....4⅜ x 10⅜ "	White or amber	22.00	11.00
No. 9-1st....4-cent... " "	White or amber	42.00	21.00
No. 10-1st....2-cent... $3\frac{9}{16}$ x 4⅝ "	White only	21.20	10.60
No. 11-1st....1-cent....4¼ x 5¼ "	White only	11.40	5.70
No. 11-1st....2-cent.... " "	White only	21.40	10.70
No. 13-1st....1-cent....3¾ x 6¾ "	White or amber	11.40	5.70
No. 13-2d.....1-cent.... " "	Buff or blue	11.20	5.60
No. 13-1st....2-cent.... " "	White or amber	21.40	10.70
No. 13-2d.....2-cent.... " "	Buff or blue	21.20	10.60
No. 14-1st. ..2-cent....3¾ x $6\frac{5}{16}$ "	White or amber	21.40	10.70
No. 14-2d.....2-cent.... " "	Buff or blue	21.20	10.60

Table Showing Number of Envelopes Cut from Sheet. Any Given Size.

PAPER SIZE.	BARONIALS.			COMMERCIALS.							
	4	5	6	5	6¼	6½	6¾	9	10	11	12
16 x 21.........	6	5	4	6	5	4	4	..	..	..	..
17 x 22.........	6	6	4	6	6	5	5	4	3	2	2
17 x 28.........	8	8	..	9	7	6	5	..	..	..	..
19 x 24.........	8	7	6	8	7	6	6	..	..	..	..
18 x 23.........	7	6	5	6	6	5	5	..	..	..	..

Envelope Manufacturing, Your Stock :

Sizes 3 to 6¾,
Also Baronials 4, 5 and 6, } Any quantity from 1 to 100,000, 40 cents per 1,000.

Official Sizes, 9 to 12 : Any quantity from 1 to 100,000, $1.00 per 1,000

40

PRINTING ENVELOPES.

PRINTER'S PRICES.

1,000 lots .... 60 cents per M.
5,000 " .... 50 "
10,000 " .... 40 "
25,000 " .... 35 "
50,000 " .... 30 "

Add 10 cents per 1,000 for colored ink.

MILL PRICES.

				Black.	Colored Ink.
3 to	5,000 lots			50 cents.	65 cents.
5 "	10,000 "			30 "	40 "
10 "	15,000 "			20 "	30 "
15 "	25,000 "			15 "	25 "
25 "	50,000 "			10 "	20 "
50 "	100,000 "			8 "	15 "
Over	100,000 "			5 "	10 "

Printing on back or seal side after envelopes have been folded—*i. e.*, printing across the flap—15 cents more per 1,000 than printing on face.

TINTING FROM TINT BLOCK.
(One Color.)

1 to 5,000 lots .... 75 cents.
10,000 " .... 50 "
20,000 " .... 40 "
25,000 " .... 35 "
50,000 " .... 30 "
100,000 " .... 25 "

Prices exclusive of cost of engraving.

To make a good job of tinting, stock must be printed flat.

Imprinting under flap, customer's own die, plain, no color, 15 cents per 1,000.

No charge is made by the manufacturers on fine correspondence papers and weddings.

41

PADDING (Johnson Process).

PADS.

$4\frac{1}{2}$ x $8\frac{1}{2}$ ⎫
$5\frac{1}{2}$ x $8\frac{1}{2}$ ⎬ ....1$\frac{1}{2}$c. each.
6 x $9\frac{1}{2}$ ⎭
7 x $8\frac{1}{2}$

In lots of 50 or over............................ 1c. each.
$8\frac{1}{2}$ x 11 ⎫ .... 2c. each.
$9\frac{1}{2}$ x 12 ⎭
In lots of 50 or over........................1$\frac{3}{4}$c. each.

For collated pads add 1c. per 100 collations.

PUNCHING.
$\frac{1}{8}$ TO $\frac{3}{8}$ INCH HOLE.

1,000 to 10,000. ....10c. per 1,000 holes.
10,000 to 20,000..................... 8c. "   "   "
20,000 to 30,000..................... 7c. "   "   "
30,000 to 50,000..................... 5c. "   "   "

EYELETTING.
REGULAR SIZES, $\frac{1}{8}$ TO $\frac{3}{8}$ INCH.

1,000 lots............................... 50c. per 1,000
10,000 " .... 45c. "   "
20,000 " .... 40c. "   "

CALENDAR EYELETS.
Card up to 11 x 14.

1,000................................... $1.25
5,000................................... 1.00 per 1,000
10,000................................... .75 "   "

ROUND CORNERING.
Ordinary Cards Up to 8-Ply Not Larger than 4 x 8.

1,000........ ....@ 50 cents.
3,000.................................. ......@ 45 cents per 1,000.
5,000...... ....@ 40 cents per 1,000.
10,000........... ....@ 30 cents per 1,000.

NUMBERING.

1,000 numbers		25 cents.	
5,000 "		20 "	per 1,000
10,000 "		18 "	"
100,000 "		15 "	"

Numbering Bank Pass Books.
Cover and inside, 60 cents. per 1,000 numbers.

Numbering Bound Books.
50 cents per 1,000 numbers.

Numbering, Perforating and Binding Insurance Policies.
Numbering, 25 cents per 1,000 numbers.
Perforating, 17 cents per 1,000 perforations.
Binding, 50 each, 4 cents per pad.
    "   100 " 5 "   "
Printing agent's name on policies, 75 cents per lot, 1,000 or less.

PERFORATING.

1,000 perforations, 25c. per 1,000 perforations.
Large quantities, 20c. "   "   "

PERFORATING BOUND BOOKS.
50 cents per 1,000 perforations.

BEVELING.

1,000 lots	90c.	
3,000 "	80c.	per 1,000
5,000 "	75c.	" "
10,000 "	70c.	" "

GOLD BEVELING.

1,000	$1.25	
3,000	1.15	per 1,000
5,000	1.00	" "
10,000	.90	" "

These prices are figured on a basis of a card 3½ x 5½.

BLOTTER CUTTING.

12 to 19 x 24,

1 Ream, 35 cents.
3 Reams, 30 cents per ream.
5 Reams, 25 cents per ream.

LABEL CUTTING.

Any Design—Hearts, Diamond, Clubs, Spades, Seals and Circles.

Designs and Circles up to 6 inches {1,000 lots, 20 cents.
{5,000 lots, 10 cents.

12-inch Circles.................. {1,000 lots, 25 cents.
{5,000 lots, 15 cents.

16-inch Circles.................. {1,000 lots, 40 cents.
{5,000 lots, 25 cents.

CUTTING.

LITHOGRAPHED WORK.

Any quantity, per ream........................... 20c.

PLAIN STOCK.

1 Ream....................................... 20c.
2 Reams....................................... 30c.
5 Reams....................................... 75c.

LITHOGRAPHED CARDS.

Any quantity, at 25c. per 1,000.

PLAIN STOCK.

Any quantity, per 1,000........................... 10c.

———

COLLATING.

Per 1,000.. 20c.

TINTING CHECKS.

Francis & Loutrel's Patent Safety Tints.

(Must be applied before Lithographing is done.)

Regular Check Tint Work on first and third pages, double cap or smaller, 100 to 150 impressions, 1½ *cents per impression.*

When less than 100 impressions are ordered, price of a full 100 will be charged.

Samples of these tints can be had on application to MESSRS. FRANCIS & LOUTREL, 146 William St., New York.

Smith's patent safety wave tints can be applied after lithographing is done.

Sheets any size up to 19 x 28.

$$
\begin{array}{ll}
\text{1,000 Checks} & \$1.50 \\
\text{1 Ream} & 3.00 \\
\text{5 Reams} & 2.75 \text{ per ream.} \\
\text{10 Reams} & 2.50 \quad '' \quad '' \\
\text{20 Reams} & 1.50 \quad '' \quad '' \\
\end{array}
$$

Samples of these tints can be had upon application to MESSRS. W. C. SMITH & Co., 91 Liberty Street, New York.

Price List of Typewritten Letters in Quantities.

(Headings to Be Supplied by Customer.)

Quantity.	Type-written Signature.	Fac-Simile Signature.
250	$2.50	$4.00
500	3.00	5.00
1,000	4.25	6.50
2,000	6.75	10.50
3,000	9.00	13.25
5,000	13.00	18.00

Special prices for larger quantities.

Addressing at lowest rates.

Prices subject to liberal trade discount.

DENNISON'S SHIPPING TAGS.

TRADE MARK
"NEW YORK"
PRICES PER 1,000.

1G	$0.25	5G	$0.50
1E	.40	5E	.85
1P	.90	5P	1.60
2G	.30	6G	.60
2E	.50	6E	1.00
2P	1.00	6P	1.90
3G	.35	7G	.70
3E	.60	7E	1.15
3P	1.20	7P	2.30
4G	.40	8G	.80
4E	.70	8E	1.30
4P	1.40	8P	2.75

Discount from these prices, 25 per cent.

LINEN SHIPPING TAGS.

1 L	$3.00 per 1,000	5 L	$6.25 per 1,000
2 L	3.75 " "	6 L	7.25 " "
3 L	4.50 " "	7 L	8.50 " "
4 L	5.25 " "	8 L	10.00 " "

Discount, 25 per cent.

TAG PRINTING.

1,000	50c.	10.000	20c. per 1,000
3,000	40c. per 1,000	25,000	18c. " "
5,000	25c. " "		

Above prices by courtesy of DENNISON M'F'G Co., 198 Broadway, N. Y.

Telephone, 722 Cortlandt.

SEE NEXT PAGE FOR DIAGRAM OF SIZES.

DENNISON'S
PATENT SHIPPING
TAGS.
Trade Mark
"MANILA."
"E"
Prices per 1,000.

1 E— .40

2 E— .50

3 E— .60

4 E— .70

5 E— .85

6 E— 1.00

7 E— 1.15

8 E— 1.30

Stringing and Wiring Shipping Tags.

Shipping Tags with Strings, at 25 cents; Single Wires at 30 cents, or Double Wires at 35 cents, per 1000 net, extra.

Loose cut strings, which can be easily looped on the tag after printing, furnished at 15 cents per 1,000 net.

Loose wires, 7½ inches long (for single wiring), at 15 cents per 1,000 net.

Loose wires, 12 inches long (for double wiring), at 20 cents per 1,000 net.

GUMMING.

Sheets up to 19 x 24, 1,000 sheets.................. $5.00

Larger sizes, 1 cent per one thousand square inches.

DENNISON'S GUMMED PAPER,

"Standard,"

Put up in ¼-ream packages, full package at ream price.

No.	Description	Size.	Sheet.	Quire.	Ream.
00	Both Sides Gummed	17 x 22	$0.04	$0.70	$11.00
0	Thin White........	17 x 22	.02	.25	3.75
1	Best White	17 x 22	.03	.35	4.75
1	" "	20 x 25	.04	.50	6.50
01	All Rope	20 x 24	.03	.40	6.75
02	" "	20 x 24	.03	.50	7.50
2	White....	17 x 22	.02	.30	4.00
2	"	20 x 25	.03	.45	5.50
3	Lemon, Medium...	20 x 25	.03	.40	4.50
3½	Salmon, " ...	20 x 25	.03	.40	4.50
4	Yellow, " ...	20 x 25	.03	.40	4.50
5	Blue " ...	20 x 25	.03	.40	4.50
6	Green, " ...	20 x 25	.03	.40	4.50
7	Pink, " ...	20 x 25	.03	.40	4.50
9	Cherry, " ...	20 x 25	.03	.40	4.50
10	Black, " ...	20 x 24	.04	.50	9.00
11	Salmon, Plated.....	20 x 24	.04	.65	10.50
13	Orange, "	20 x 24	.04	.65	10.50
14	Green, "	20 x 24	.04	.70	11.00
15	" Glazed.....	20 x 24	.04	.70	11.00
19	Black, Plated......	20 x 24	.04	.70	11.00
20	Vermil., "	20 x 24	.05	.70	12.75
20½	" Glazed.....	20 x 24	.05	.70	12.75
21	Steel Blue	20 x 24	.06	1.00	15.00
22	White Coated......	17 x 22	.03	.45	7.50
23	Buff, Plated	20 x 24	.04	.65	10.50
24	Lav., "	20 x 24	.04	.65	10.50
25	Pink	20 x 24	.04	.65	10.50
26	Peacock..........	20 x 24	.04	.65	10.50
27	Pearl.............	20 x 24	.04	.65	10.50
28	Nile Green........	20 x 24	.04	.65	10.50
29	Canary...........	20 x 25	.04	.65	10.50
30	Blue, Glazed.......	20 x 25	.04	.70	12.00

By courtesy of DENNISON MFG. Co., New York.

RUBBER STAMPS.

(Subject to change without notice.)

Rubber Hand Stamps, one line, not exceeding ½ x 2
inches...$0.10
Each additional line.. .05
Not exceeding ½ x 3 inches.................................... .12
Each additional line.. .07
Not exceeding ½ x 4... .15
Each additional line.. .08
Not exceeding ½ x 5 inches.................................... .17
Each additional line .... .09
Not exceeding ½ x 6 inches.................................... .20
Each additional line.. .10
   For longer lines send for estimate.

Stamps on Moulding, and Peg Stamps, according to size and inscription.

Brass Mounts, nickel-plated, one line, not exceeding
  ½ x 3 inches...$0.15
Each additional line.. .08
Not exceeding 4 inches... .20
Each additional line.. .10
   For longer lines send for estimate.
   Stamps with curved lines are double the above prices.
One line fac-simile wood-cut, not exceeding 1 x 3
  inches...$0.60
Each additional line.. .40

Rubber Stamps, from woodcut,

Not exceeding 1 x 3 inches.......................... $0.20
Each additional line................................ .10
   For sizes exceeding above, send for estimate.

STENCILS.

Roman or Gothic Letters.

	PER LETTER.
1 inch and under	$0.01½
1¼ "	.02½
1½ "	.04
1¾ "	.05
2 "	.06
2½ "	.07

Prices of Special Stencils on application.

STEEL STAMPS.

For Branding, etc.

	PER LETTER.
$\frac{1}{32}$ inch	$0.09
$\frac{1}{24}$ "	.09
$\frac{1}{20}$ "	.09
$\frac{1}{16}$ "	.09
$\frac{1}{12}$ "	.09
$\frac{1}{10}$ "	.09
$\frac{1}{8}$ "	.09
$\frac{5}{32}$ "	.11
$\frac{3}{16}$ "	.12
$\frac{1}{4}$ "	.17
$\frac{3}{8}$ "	.22
$\frac{7}{16}$ "	.27
$\frac{1}{2}$ "	.32

Forgings extra, according to size and weight.

SEAL PRESSES AND WAX SEALS.

No. 1 or 2 Lion Head
No. 00, 0, 1 or 2 Maas
No. 1 or 2 Pocket and
No. 1 Favorite Seal
   Presses ....

Plain seal, with solid composition, metal counter $1.25

Same with copper counter	1.50
No. 3 Lion Head or Maas, plain seal	3.50
Consular, plain seal	3.00
County Seal, 3 inch die, plain seal	7.50
Mammoth Seal, 3 inch die, plain seal	12.00
Wax Seals, round or oval	0.25

and upwards.

TABLE

SHOWING THE COST OF PAPER BY THE QUIRE OR HUNDRED SHEETS AT ANY GIVEN PRICE PER REAM.

Per Ream.	Per Quire.	Per 100 Sheets.	Per Ream.	Per Quire.	Per 100 Sheets.
$1.00	$0.05	$0.20	$8.25	$0.41¼	$1.72
1.25	6¼	26	8.50	42½	1.77
1.50	7½	31	8.75	43¾	1.82
1.75	8¾	36	9.00	45	1.88
2.00	10	42	9.25	46¼	1.93
2.25	11¼	47	9.50	47½	1.98
2.50	12½	52	9.75	48¾	2.03
2.75	13¾	57	10.00	50	2.08
3.00	15	62	10.25	51¼	2.14
3.25	16¼	68	10.50	52½	2.19
3.50	17½	73	10.75	53¾	2.24
3.75	18¾	78	11.00	55	2.29
4.00	20	83	11.25	56¼	2.34
4.25	21¼	89	11.50	57½	2.40
4.50	22½	94	11.75	58¾	2.45
4.75	23¾	99	12.00	60	2.50
5.00	25	1.04	12.25	61¼	2.55
5.25	26¼	1.09	12.50	62½	2.60
5.50	27½	1.15	12.75	63¾	2.65
5.75	28¾	1.20	13.00	65	2.70
6.00	30	1.25	13.25	66¼	2.76
6.25	31¼	1.30	13.50	67½	2.82
6.50	32½	1.35	13.75	68¾	2.87
6.75	33¾	1.41	14.00	70	2.92
7.00	35	1.46	14.25	71¼	2.97
7.25	36¼	1.51	14.50	72½	3.02
7.50	37½	1.56	14.75	73¾	3.07
7.75	38¾	1.61	15.00	75	3.12
8.00	40	1.67	16.00	80	3.33

TABLE

SHOWING THE NUMBER OF SHEETS REQUIRED TO CUT 1,000 PIECES.

No. on a Sheet.	No. of Sheets.	No. on a Sheet.	No. of Sheets.	No. on a Sheet.	No. of Sheets.
2	500	35	29	68	15
3	334	36	28	69	15
4	250	37	28	70	15
5	200	38	27	71	15
6	167	39	26	72	14
7	143	40	25	73	14
8	125	41	25	74	14
9	112	42	24	75	14
10	100	43	24	76	14
11	91	44	23	77	13
12	84	45	23	78	13
13	77	46	22	79	13
14	72	47	22	80	13
15	67	48	21	81	13
16	63	49	21	82	13
17	59	50	20	83	13
18	56	51	20	84	12
19	53	52	20	85	12
20	50	53	19	86	12
21	48	54	19	87	12
22	46	55	19	88	12
23	44	56	18	89	12
24	42	57	18	90	12
25	40	58	18	91	11
26	39	59	17	92	11
27	38	60	17	93	11
28	36	61	17	94	11
29	35	62	17	95	11
30	34	63	16	96	11
31	33	64	16	97	11
32	32	65	16	98	11
33	31	66	16	99	11
34	30	67	15	100	10

TYPE RULE FOR MEASURING .. .. COMPOSITION

5 POINT measures 15 ems to the inch.

5½ POINT measures 13 ems to the inch.

6 POINT measures 12 ems to the inch.

8 POINT measures 9 ems to the inch.

10 POINT measures 7⅓ ems to the inch.

12 POINT measures 6 ems to the inch.

To get number of ems in a page, multiply the square of the type page by the square of the ems in an inch.

EXAMPLE:

> Size of page, 5 inches wide × 6 inches long =30 square inches.
>
> Type, 12 point=6 ems to inch=(square) 36 ems.
>
> Square of page (30) × square of type (36) =1,080 ems to page.

NOTE.—4½ point, which measures 16 ems to the inch; 7 point, which measures 10 ems to the inch; 9 point, which measures 8 ems to the inch, and 11 point, which measures 6 3-5 ems to the inch, are not set in scale, as they are little used.

MOURNING BORDERS.

No. 5. No. 4. No. 3. No. 2. No. 1. Italian.

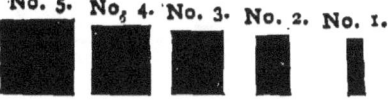

NUMBERS—Styles and Sizes.

A
34671.

D
215629

F
D825603

H
★135740

I
32567

J
15924

L
73561

M
25478

N
217456

55

A
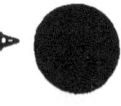

B

1

4

7

9

13

17

21

25

29

33

39

46

104.
103
102.
101
100
99.
98.

98 is Gentlemens Club Small.
99 " " " Large.
100 " " Small.
101 " " Large.
102 " Miss Small Oblong
103 " Mrs. " "
104 " Mr. & Mrs. " "

204.
203
202.
201
200.

200 is Miss Small
201 " " Large
202 " Mrs. Small
203 " " Large
204 " Mr. & Mrs. or Reception.

STANDARD SIZES AND WEIGHTS OF MANILA PAPERS.

SCALE OF WEIGHTS EQUAL TO 24 x 36.

SIZE.	15	20	25	30	35	40	50	60	70	80	90	100	125	150
24 x 36	15	20	25	30	35	40	50	60	70	80	90	100	125	150
12 x 18	4	5	6	8	9	10	13	15	18	20	23	25	31	38
15 x 20	5	7	9	11	12	14	18	21	24	28	31	35	44	52
18 x 24	8	10	13	15	18	20	25	30	35	40	45	50	63	75
20 x 30	11	14	18	21	25	28	35	42	49	56	63	70	87	105
22 x 32	12	16	20	25	29	33	40	50	57	65	74	80	102	120
26 x 36	16	22	27	33	38	44	54	65	76	87	98	109	136	163
30 x 40	21	28	35	42	49	56	70	84	97	112	125	140	174	209
36 x 40	25	34	42	50	59	67	84	100	117	134	150	167	209	250
40 x 48	34	45	56	67	78	90	112	133	156	180	200	224	278	336
48 x 52	44	58	72	87	101	116	144	174	202	232	261	288	360	432
48 x 64	54	71	89	107	125	142	178	214	250	284	321	356	445	534

STANDARD SIZES OF BOOK PAPERS.

22 x 28	26 x 40
23 x 33	26 x 38
24 x 36	28 x 42
24 x 38	28 x 44
25 x 38	33 x 46

30½ x 41

Book Papers range in price from 3¼ cents to 7 cents per pound.

STANDARD SIZES AND WEIGHTS OF WOODCUT, COATED PAPER.

22 x 28...........	40, 50, 60, 70, 80, 90, 100 lbs.
25 x 38...........	60, 70, 80, 90, 100, 120 lbs.
28 x 42...........	70, 80, 90, 100, 120 lbs.
33 x 46...........	100, 120 lbs.
Colored, 25 x 40..	100 lbs.

BINDERS' BOARDS.

NO. 2 GRADE.

	Per Ton.
Mediums, 22 x 26, Nos. 18 to 60.................	$
Double Caps, 20 x 30, 18 to 60	35.00
No. 1 Davy's	100.00

(40 bdls to ton.)

TRUNK BOARDS.

34 x 44, No. 4 to 14, No. 2 grade......	$35.00 per ton.
No. 1 Davy's.......................	3.50 per bundle.

PAPER SIZES.

Name.	Size.	Weight.
Flat Letter	10 x 16	7 to 12 lbs.
Pot Cap	12½ x 15½	10 "
Typewriter Cap	13 x 16	5 to 12 "
Flat Cap	14 x 17	12 to 20 "
Crown	15 x 19	18 to 24 "
Demy	16 x 21	18 to 30 "
Folio	17 x 22	12 to 28 "
Check Folio	17½ x 24	20 to 24 "
Medium	18 x 23	24 to 40 "
Royal	19 x 24	20 to 44 "
New Sizes	19 x 26	28 to 32 "
White and Colored	19 x 23	32 to 36 "
Wedding Royal	20 x 24	40 "
" Folio	21 x 33	50 to 80 "
Super Royal	20 x 28	36 to 54 "
Imperial	23 x 31	72 "
Double Letter	16 x 20	18 to 24 "
" Typewriter	16 x 26	10 to 24 "
" Cap	17 x 28	24 to 40 "
" Crown	19 x 30	36 to 44 "
" Demy	16 x 42	56 to 60 "
" "	21 x 32	40 to 60 "
" Folio	22 x 34	28 to 48 "
" Medium	18 x 46	72 to 80 "
" "	23 x 36	72 to 80 "
" Royal	24 x 38	88 "
" Elephant	27 x 40	125 "
" Double Cap	28 x 34	56 to 80 "
Book and News	22 x 28	30 to 80 "
" "	23 x 41	35 to 80 "
" "	24 x 38	30 to 120 "
" "	26 x 40	35 to 100 "
" "	28 x 42	35 to 100 "
" "	33 x 46	50 to 120 "
Blotting, thin	17 x 28	"
" "	18 x 23	"
" "	20 x 24	"
" thick	19 x 24	60 to 140 "
Tinted Cover	20 x 25	22 to 80 "
" "	22 x 28	31 to 100 "
" "	23 x 33	40 "
Glazed "	20 x 24	"
Marbled Medium	20 x 25	"
" Double Cap	19½ x 30	"
Manila Wrapping	20 x 30	15 to 60 "
" "	22 x 32	20 to 60 "
" "	24 x 36	20 to 100 "
" "	30 x 40	30 to 120 "
" "	40 x 48	50 to 200 "
" "	48 x 64	150 to 250 "
Card Board	22 x 28	100 to 180 "
Press Board	21 x 31	60 to 70 "
" "	24 x 32	60 to 180 "
" "	30 x 40	350 "
" "	31 x 44	350 "
Tar Board	22 x 27	No. 15 to 50
" "	21 x 30½	No. 15 to 50
Wood Board	26 x 38	No. 20 to 120
Straw Board	26 x 38	No. 15 to 150

MANILA COPYING PAPER.

Size.	Description.	Price Per Ream.
20½ x 24½	Thin Quality, long fold	$2.60
20½ x 28½	" " "	3.00
20½ x 24½	"Electric" quality, long fold	2.80
20½ x 30½	" " "	4.50
20½ x 24½	"Parchment" quality (heavy), long fold	4.80
20½ x 28½	" " " "	5.40
24½ x 30½	" " (medium), flat...	6.50

UNGLAZED COPYING PAPER.

Size.	Description.	Price Per Ream.
18 x 22	White or buff, long fold	$2.40
20½ x 24½	" " "	3.20
20½ x 28½	" " "	4.00

JAPANESE COPYING PAPER.

Size.	Description.	Price Per Ream.
18 x 22	Watermarked "JAP," long fold	$3.60
19 x 24	" " "	4.25
20½ x 24½	" " "	4.75
20 x 28	" " "	5.25
20½ x 30½	" " "	6.00
19 x 32	" " broad fold	5.35

TOKIO.

Size.	Description.	Price Per Ream.
20½ x 24½	Long fold	$9.00
20½ x 14½	Broad "	6.00

FUJIYAMA.

Size.	Description.	Price Per Ream.
20½ x 24½	Long fold	$10.00
20½ x 14½	Broad "	7.00
19 x 24	" "	9.75

WHITE SILK COPYING PAPER.

Size.	Description.	Price Per Ream.
18 x 22	Watermarked "1548," long fold	$3.60
20½ x 24½	" " "	4.75
20½ x 28½	" " "	5.75
20½ x 30½	" " "	6.00

Discount, 60 per cent.
BOORUM & PEASE COMPANY, 101 Duane St., New York.

TABLE FOR COMPUTING COMPARA-TIVE WEIGHTS OF FLAT PAPERS.

The number of square inches in the sheet weight known, multi-plied by the weight per square inch of the sheet weight not known, gives comparative weight of sheet unknown.

Size.	Weight.	No. of Square Inches in Sheet.	Weight per Square Inch.
15 x 19...............	18	285	.0631 lbs.
"	20	285	.0702 "
"	22	285	.0772 "
"	24	285	.0842 "
16 x 21...............	16	336	.0476 "
"	18	336	.0533 "
"	20	336	.0594 "
"	22	336	.0655 "
"	24	336	.0714 "
"	26	336	.0773 "
"	28	336	.0833 "
"	30	336	.0892 "
17 x 22...................	14	374	.0374 "
"	16	374	.0428 "
"	18	374	.0481 "
"	20	374	.0535 "
"	22	374	.0588 "
"	24	374	.0642 "
"	26	374	.0695 "
"	28	374	.0748 "
17 x 28...................	20	476	.042 "
"	24	476	.0504 "
"	28	476	.0588 "
"	32	476	.0672 "
"	36	476	.0756 "
"	40	476	.084 "
18 x 23...................	20	414	.0483 "
"	24	414	.0579 "
"	28	414	.0676 "
"	30	414	.0724 "
"	32	414	.0773 "
"	36	414	.087 "
"	40	414	.0966 "
19 x 24...................	20	456	.0438 "
"	22	456	.0482 "
"	24	456	.0526 "
"	28	456	.0614 "
"	30	456	.0658 "
"	32	456	.0702 "
"	36	456	.0789 "
"	40	456	.0877 "
"	44	456	.0964 "
20 x 28.	36	560	.0643 "
"	54	560	.0964 "
23 x 31...................	48	713	.0673 "
"	72	713	.101 "
21 x 33.....	50	693	.0721 "
"	60	693	.0865 "
"	70	693	.101 "
"	80	693	.115 "
23 x 28...................	65	644	.101 "
23 x 34...................	80	762	.102 "
26 x 33...................	100	858	.119 "
27 x 40..	125	1080	.115 "
31 x 53...................	200	1643	.121 "
48 x 72...............	500	3456	.145 "

INDEX TO TRADE DIRECTORY.

TRADE DIRECTORY.

BLANK-BOOK BINDERS.

Albers, William F., & Bro., 60 Maiden Lane; telephone, Cort'd 2759.

Anderson, Prigge & Anderson, 206 Centre St.; telephone, Spring 1053.

Austin & Magill, 155 Fulton St.; telephone.

Beckett & Bradford Co., 35 Vesey St.; telephone, Cort'd 2272.

Bloodgood, Andrew D., 158 William St.; telephone.

Brunworth, Munn & Barber, 53 E. 10th St.; telephone, 18th St. 1631.

Brassil, Daniel S., 409 Pearl St.; telephone.

Cassidy, John, 221 Fulton St.; telephone, Cort'd 3406.

Chapman & Co., 48 Broad St.; telephone.

Connolly, J. B., 156 William St.; telephone, John 742.

Davis & Fitzgerald, 7 Dutch St.; telephone, Cort'd 813.

Dannerlein & Merk, 13 Stone St.; telephone.

English, James H., & Son, 60 Murray St.; telephone, Cort'd 4216.

Foster & Nolen, 40 Cortlandt St.; telephone.

Gafney, Joseph, 81 John St.; telephone.

Gafney & Jackson, 71 John St.; telephone.

Johnston, Samuel, 2 Liberty St.; telephone.

Johnston, Wm. G., & Co., 51 Franklin St.; telephone.

Kendig, B. F., 91 Liberty St.; telephone.

Kissam, B. A., 25 Beekman St.; telephone.

Lefferts, Harry T., 47 Broad St.; telephone.

L'Enfant, Chas., 142 Fifth Ave.

Middleton, Maire, 143 Fulton St.

Nelson, G. E., 58 John St.; telephone.

Pakenham & Dowling, 12 Spruce St.; telephone.

Reilly & Eagle, 49 John St.—Cort'd 2256.

Rosenzweig, Son & Co., 67 Park Place; telephone, Cort'd 2529.

Smigel, Isaac, 166 William St.; telephone, John 874.

Stratton, Chas. A., Co., 42 Beaver St.; telephone, Broad 2507.

Stratton, Wm. A., 70 Pine St.; telephone, John 1591.

Wood & Salter, 12 Dutch St.; telephone, Cort'd 2740.

PAMPHLET AND MAGAZINE BINDERS.

Buckley & Wood, 52 Duane St.; telephone, Fr'klin 829.

Cortelyou, Henry, 21 Vandewater St. ; telephone.

Gardiner Binding & Mailing Co., 218 William St. ; telephone, John 1934.

Knoepke, William, Pamphlet Binding Co., 45 Rose St. ; 30 Lafayette Place ; telephone, John 1607.

Levenson, Max, & Son, 211 Centre St. ; telephone, Spring 2301.

Miller & Drummond, 23 Vandewater St. ; telephone.

Shaljian & Powell, 39 Gold St. ; telephone, John 777.

Waters, W., & Son, 103 Fulton St.; telephone, Cort'd 3162.

BLANK BOOK MANUFACTURERS.

Boorum & Pease Co., 103 Duane St.; telephone, Fr'klin 15.

Corlies Blank Book Co., 172 Centre St.; telephone.

Kiggins & Tooker Co., 123 William St.; telephone, Cort'd 4294.

Liebenroth, Von Auw & Co., 23 E. Houston St.; telephone, Spring 1410.

National Blank Book Co., 52 Duane St.; telephone, Fr'klin 922.

New York Blank Book Co., 9 Laight St.; telephone, Fr'klin 1699.

Rubel Bros., 190 W. Broadway ; telephone, Fr'klin 683.

Saugerties Mfg. Co., 54 Franklin St.; telephone.

Shaw, J. G., Blank Book Co , 261 Canal St.; telephone, Spring 1099.

Slote, Daniel & Co., 119 William St.; telephone.

Vernon, S. E. & M., 69 Duane St.; telephone, Fr'klin 1031.

BOOK HEADING PRINTERS.

De Baun, Peter, & Co., 156 William St., telephone.

Heinrich, F., 206 Centre St.; telephone.

Moore & Warren, 57 John St., telephone, Cortlandt 604.

Smith & Clauson, 23 Beekman St.

ENVELOPE DEALERS AND MANUFACTURERS.

Barnum & Co., 120 William St. ; telephone.
Berlin & Jones Envelope Co., 136 William St. ; telephone.
Clasp Envelope Co., West Broadway; telephone, John 81.
Commercial Envelope Co., 97 6th Ave.
Connecticut Valley Paper and Envelope Co., 57 Beekman
    St. ; telephone, John 925.
Kantor, A. A., 194 William St.
Nesbitt, Geo. F., & Co., 167 Pearl St.—John 1279.
Raynon & Perkins Envelope Co., 115 William St. ; telephone, Cort'd 489.
Straub Envelope Co., 27 Beekman St.—John 1817.
Tension Envelope Co., 28 Reade St. ; telephone.

ENGRAVERS—COPPER, STEEL AND DIE.

Alford, H. G., & Co., 96 Fulton St.; 'phone, John 685.
Bishop, Wm., & Son, corner William and John Sts.
Clark, Francis, 178 Broadway ; telephone.
Dietz, Adolph R., 58 Ann St.; telephone.
McCarthy, Thomas F., 22 Spruce St., telephone.
Noble & Brown, 10 Warren St.; telephone, Cortl'dt 4780.
Ridley, Samuel C., 87 Fulton St.
Stationers' Engraving Co., 507 W. Broadway; telephone,
    Spring 2529.
Turner Bros., 116 William St.; telephone.
Wiltshire, Harry, 120 Fulton St.; telephone, Cort'd 1078.

ENGRAVERS—MAP AND CHART.

Bonnay & Co., 61 Beekman St.; telephone.
Bradley & Poates, 12 Vandewater St.; telephone, John 1676.
Bridgman, E. C., 84 Warren St.; telephone.
Cotton, Ohman & Co., 15 Warren St.; telephone.
Fisk, E. F., 96 Fulton St.; telephone.
McLeese, Frank, & Bros., 218 William St.; telephone.
Rand, McNally & Co., 142 Fifth Ave.; telephone, 18th
    St. 1250.
Servoss, R. D., 18 Murray St.; telephone.

ENGRAVERS—BANK NOTE.

Kihn & Hall, 111 Liberty St.; telephone, Cort'd 5336.
McCaski, G. T. & F., 110 Liberty St.; telephone.
Noble & Brown, 10 Warren St.—Cort'd 4780.
(See any bank-note company).

ENGRAVERS—WAX.

McLees, Frank & Brothers, 218 William St.; telephone.

ENGRAVERS—MUSIC.

Fritz, Albert, 448 Sixth Ave.; telephone.
Fruin, R. F., 2 Union Square, E.; telephone.
Hounslow, W. E., 126 Bible House; telephone.
Lawson, Frank J., 212 E. 9th St.; telephone.
Passow, M., 73 Third Ave.; telephone.
Pearson, J. O., 73 Third Ave.; telephone.
Simermeyer, F., 218 E. 9th St.; telephone.
Feller, R., Sons & Dorn, 224 W. 26th St.; telephone.

ENGRAVERS—PHOTO.

Butt, Chas., 112 Fulton St.; telephone.
Central Bureau of Engraving, 157 William St.—Cort'd 3469.
Enterprise Engraving Co., 102 Fulton St.; telephone.
Manhattan Photo-Eng. Co., 11 New Chambers St.; telephone, Fr'klin 1657.
New York Engraving and Printing Co., 320 Pearl St.—John 97.
Rigler, F. A., Co., 26 Park Place; telephone, Cort'd 944.

ENGRAVERS—WOOD.

Butt, Chas., 112 Fulton St.; telephone.
Cox Engraving Co., 108 Fulton St.; telephone.
Field & Beattie, 89 Fulton St.; telephone, John 645.
N. Y. Woodcut Co., 293 Broadway.
Miller, Charles A. D., 82 Nassau St.

NUMBERERS, PERFORATORS, BOOK PAGERS AND INDEXING.

See blank-book binders; also,
J. B. Connolly, 156 William St.; telephone, John 742.
Fitzpatrick Bros., 102 John St.; telephone.
Harris, E. A. & W., 83 John St.; telephone.
Hickey, J. J., 101 Maiden Lane; telephone.
Hindle, J. B., 26 Church St.; telephone.
Moore & Warren, 57 John St.; telephone, Cort'd 604.
Smigel, Isaac, 166 William St.; telephone, John 874.

PADDERS.

(See Binders and)
J. B. Connolly, 156 William St.; telephone, John 742.
Shoemaker & Comskey, 103 Fulton St.

PAPER CUTTERS.

Connolly, J. B., 156 William St.; telephone, John 742.
Shoemaker & Comiskey, 103 Fulton St.
Young, B. F., 26 Beekman St.; telephone.

CARD CUTTERS, BEVELERS AND ROUND CORNERERS.

(See Cardboard Dealers.)

PAPER RULERS.

See Blank-Book Binders, and
Arnold & Kolde, 64 Fulton St.; telephone.
Berman & Ackley, 10 Reade St.; telephone.
Chapman & Co., 48 Broad St.; telephone.
Cowen, James E., 62 Broad St.; telephone.
Gilbert & Beecher, 24 Reade St.
Horan & Armet, 61 Warren St.
Male, I., & Sons, 53 Crosby St.; 'phone, Spring 2035.
Shoemaker & Comiskey, 103 Fulton St.
Smith, Peter, 54 Beekman St.—John 907.
Vanhouten Bros., 275 Pearl St.

LITHOGRAPHERS—COMMERCIAL.

Gaul & Topp, 22 Vesey St.; telephone.

Kinscherf, C., 27 Beckman St.; telephone, Cort'd 1465.

Klim, Linder & Bauer Litho. Co., 411 Pearl St.; telephone, John 1924.

Knickerbocker Litho. Co., 97 Maiden Lane.

Powers, W. F., & Co., 25 City Hall Place; telephone, Fr'klin 1541.

Schmolze, Chas., 2 Duane St.; telephone, John 1864.

Schmolze & Hildenbrand, 16 Vandewater St.; telephone, John 1222.

PHOTOLITHOGRAPHERS.

Leggo Bros. & Co., 32 Park Place; telephone.

TRADE PRINTERS.

Bain, Burns & Barkley, 67 Park Place; telephone, 352 Cortlandt.

Bruen, E. C., 100 Nassau St.; telephone, Cort'dt 2325.

Burr Printing House, Frankfort and Jacob Sts.—John 316.

Burtard, A. M., Co., 157 William St.—Cort'dt 8596.

Chambers Printing Co., 30 New Chambers St.—John 1536.

Cherouny Printing & Pub. Co., 21 Vandewater St.—John 1678.

De Baun, Peter, & Co., 156 William St.

De Vinne, Theodore L., & Co., 12 Lafayette Place.—Spring 290.

Leach, Henry W. B., 88 Fulton St.—John 801.

McBreen & Sons, 216-218 William St.; telephone, 1615 John.

Shepherd's, C., Sons, 152 Worth St.

Stettiner Bros., 52 Duane St.—Fr'klin 1067.

Trunk Bros., 95 William St.

PHOTO-GELATINE PRINTERS.

Albertype Co., 250 Adams St., Brooklyn; telephone, 1978 Brooklyn.

STAMPERS—ON LEATHER, ETC.

Koven, W., Jr., 16 Spruce St.; telephone.
Walcutt, Bros., 143 Centre St.; telephone, Frk'ln 565.
(See Blank-Book Binders.)

STAMPERS—DIE.

(See Steel and Copper Plate Engravers.)

STEEL AND COPPER PLATE PRINTERS.

(See Steel and Copper Plate Engravers.)

TAGS AND PIN TICKETS.

Cunningham, J. G., 338 Broadway.
Dennison Mfg. Co., 198 Broadway; 'phone, Cort'd 722.
Eisler, Anthony & Co., 227 Canal St.
Kimball, A., Co., 309 W. Broadway; 'phone, Spring 158.
Rayburn Mfg. Co., 72 Duane St.
Sailsbury Mfg. Co., 695 Broadway.
Spencer Tag Co., 419 Broome St.
Thomas Mfg. Co., 18 Reade St.
Van Wagenen, Herbert, 159 Duane St.; 'phone, Fr'klin 294.

TAG ENVELOPES.

Spencer Tag Co., 419 Broome St.

STATIONERS—WHOLESALE.

Bainbridge, Henry, & Co., 101 William St.
Kimpton, Edward, 48 John St.
Tower Mfg. & Novelty Co., 306 Broadway.—Fr'klin 693.

LEAD PENCILS.

American Lead Pencil Co., 491 Broadway.—Spring 176.
Bert, Richard, 63 Duane St.
Blaisdell Paper Pencil Co., 346 Broadway.
Dixon, Joseph, Crucible Co., 68 Reade St.—Fr'klin 372.
Eagle Pencil Co., 377 Broadway.—Fr'klin 871.
Faber, A. W., 78 Reade St.—Fr'klin 1212.
Faber, Eberhard, 545 Pearl St.—Fr'klin 726.
Hardtmuth, L. V. C., 123 W. Houston.
Lany & Scherer, 46 E. 8th St.
Leman, Geo. W., & Bro., 51 Fulton.
Richert, J. William, 215 Bowery.

PENS, STEEL.

Barnes, A. S., & Co., 156 Fifth Ave.—18th St. 1714.
Crawford, J., & Co., 10 John St.
Dewolf, Hayman S., 536 E. 88th St.
Electric Pen Co., 63 E. 8th St.
Esterbrook Steel Pen Mfg. Co., 26 John St.—Cort'dt 4613.
Gillott, Joseph, & Sons, 91 John St.
Hoe, Henry, 91 John St.
Isaacs, A. L., 62 Liberty St.
Isaacs, Leon, & Co., 62 Liberty St.
Leman, Geo. W., & Bro., 51 Fulton St.
Miller Bros. Cutlery Co., 332 Broadway.—Fr'klin 574.
Oppenheimer, J., Elm and Worth Sts.
Sadler, Lee R., 752 West End Ave.
Salomon, Abram L., 177 Broadway.
Spencerian Pen Co., 450 Broome St.

INK AND MUCILAGE MANUFACT-URERS.

Barnes National Ink Co., 56 E. 10th St.
Carters Ink Co., 438 Pearl St.; 'phone, Fr'klin 1335.
Caws Pen and Ink Co., 168 Broadway.
Davids, Thaddeus, Co., 127 William St.
Davis, Emry, 41 Park Row.
Keller, Paul H., 228 E. 24th St.
Oppenheimer, Jacob, 422 E. 76th St.
Perce Manufacturing Co., 120 Liberty St.
Russell, W. S., 198 Elm St.
Safety Bottle and Ink Co., 283 Pearl St.
Sanford Manufacturing Co., 131 William St.—Cort'dt 657.
Stafford, Samuel S., 605 Washington St.—Spring 1203.
Underwood, John, & Co., 30 Vesey St.—Cort'dt 647.

MANILA AND WRAPPING PAPER DEALERS.

Coy, Hunt & Co., 72 Duane St.; 'phone, Fr'klin 2044.
Hubbs, Chas. F., & Co., 36 Beckman St.—Cort'dt 704.
Jones & Skinner, 131 William St.—Cort'dt 5220.
Millar, Geo. W., & Co., 62 Duane St.—Fr'klin 2254.
Walton, D. S., & Co., 132 Franklin St.—Fr'klin 509.

CARDBOARD DEALERS.

Bahrenburg & Co., 29 Beekman St. ; telephone, 531 Cortlandt.

Clement & Stockwell, 30 Beekman St. ; telephone, 441 Cortlandt.

Dane, William P., 174 William St. ; telephone, 511 John.

Grady, Joseph I., 31 Beekman St., telephone, 2658 Cortlandt.

Hurd, Geo. B., & Co., 425-427 Broome St. ; telephone, 723 Spring.

Linde, J. E., Paper Co., 214-218 William St. ; telephone, 1941 John.

Phœnix Card & Paper Co., 47 Beekman St. ; telephone, 462 John.

Scarborough, E. W., & Co., 28 Beekman St. ; telephone, 3200 Cortlandt.

Simpson, Geo. H., & Co., 8 Spruce St., telephone, 81 Cortlandt.

Standard Card & Paper Co., 27 Beekman St. ; telephone, 5045 Cortlandt.

Union Card & Paper Co., 27 Beekman St.; telephone, 2374 Cortlandt.

Whiting Paper Co., 148-152 Duane St. ; telephone, 554 Franklin.

Williams, Chas. W., & Co., 29 Beekman St. ; telephone, 3225 Cortlandt.

PAPER DEALERS.

American News Co., 39-41 Chambers St., Telephone 1964 Franklin.

Anderson, J. F., Jr., Co., 34 Beekman St., Telephone 172 Cortlandt.

Bainbridge, C. T., & Sons, 2 Cumberland St., Telephone 41 Main Brooklyn.

Bates, Hayden, J., & Co., 150 Nassau St.

Berlin & Jones Envelope Co., 134 William St., Telephone 81 John.

Clement & Stockwell, 30 Beekman St., Telephone 441 Cortlandt.

Conrow Brothers, 33 Beekman St., Telephone 1553 Cortlandt.

Dane, William P., 174 William St., Telephone 511 John.

Flinn, F. A., 32 Beekman St., Telephone 1194 Cortlandt.

Hake, P. H., Mfg. Co., 132-134 Essex St., Telephone 1233 A Spring.

Hard, Melvin T., 25 Beekman St., Telephone 2212 Cortlandt.

Hasbrouck, W. H. & Co.

Hurd, Geo. B., & Co., 425-427 Broome St., Telephone 723 Spring.

Junger Paper Co., 30 Bond St., Telephone 214 Spring.

Kastner, R. C.

King, Albert B., & Co., 105 William St., Telephone 3717 Cortlandt.

La Monte, George B., 87 Maiden Lane, Telephone 1649 John.

Liebenroth, Von Amo.

Linde, J. E., Paper Co., 214 William St., Telephone 1941 John.

Lindenmeyer, Henry, & Sons, 20 Beekman St., Telephone 224 Cortlandt; Bleecker and Mott Sts., Telephone 1843 Spring.

Merriam, E. J., 23 Beekman St., Telephone 1209 Cortlandt.

PAPER DEALERS—Continued.

Miller, Sloane & Wright, 65-67 Duane St., Telephones 74 Franklin and 1329 Franklin.

Molleson Brothers & Co., 18 Beekman St., Telephone 842 Cortlandt.

Phœnix Card and Paper Co., 47 Beekman St., Telephone 462 John.

Plummer, M., & Co., 45 Beekman St., Telephone 515 John.

Pirie, Alexander, & Sons, 33 Rose St.

Raynor & Perkins Envelope Co., 115 William St., Telephone 489 Cortlandt.

Sarle, John F., 58 John St., Telephone 185 Cortlandt.

Scarborough, E. W., Co., 28 Beekman St., Telephone 3200 Cortlandt.

Simpson, Geo. H., 8 Spruce St., Telephone 81 Cortlandt.

Standard Card and Paper Co., 27 Beekman St., Telephone 5045 Cortlandt.

Syndicate Trading Co., 2 Walker St., Telephone 659 Franklin.

Tower Mfg. Co., 306 Broadway, Telephone 693 Franklin.

Union Card and Paper Co., 27 Beekman St., Telephone 2374 Cortlandt.

Vernon Brothers Co., 22 Reade St., Telephone 832 B Franklin.

Walker, J. H., 16-18 Reade St., Telephone 1205 Franklin.

Ward, Marcus, & Co., 310 Sixth Ave., Telephone 860 18th St.

Watkins, J. P., 9-15 Murray St., Telephone 1155 Cortlandt.

Whiting Paper Co., 148 Duane St., Telephone 554 Franklin.

Williams, Chas. W., & Co., 29 Beekman St., Telephone 3225 Cortlandt.

Wyckoff, Seaman & Benedict. 327 Broadway, Telephone 2080 Franklin.

*Full list of watermarked and brand papers, with prices
of same, carried in stock by the New York dealers.
In lots of less than a ream add one cent per pound, and in
large lots get direct quotations.
For addresses and telephone calls of these dealers see list
of Paper dealers in trade directory.
Papers marked * thus, not watermarked.
Hurd's and Whiting's ream prices subject to 20% discount.
"S" as price mark means controlled by a Stationer. No
price quoted.
"N" as price mark means not quoted.*

A

* A Blue Fine. Vernon Bros. & Co	$0.10
* A Mills. Vernon Bros. & Co	.08
Aberdeen Linen. Phœnix Card & Paper Co	.11
Advance Linen Ledger. All dealers	.18
* Aetna Mills. F. A. Flinn	.09½
Agawam. Ex. Superfine. Miller, Sloan & Wright	.13
Agawam Bond. Miller, Sloan & Wright	List
Ajax. E. J. Merriam	.14
Alberta Bond. Geo. H. Simpson & Co	.11
* Albion Mills. Raynor & Perkins Envelope Co	N
* Alert Mills. Conrow Bros	.06
Alexis Bond. J. F. Anderson, Jr. & Co	.16
Alexis Linen Ledger. J. F. Anderson, Jr. & Co	.15
* Alligator. Geo. B. Hurd & Co. 21 x 33. Ream,	18.75
American Linen Typewriter Paper. Raynor & Perkins Envelope Co	N
* American Mills. Melvin T. Hard	.14
Anchor Linen. Geo. H. Simpson & Co	.07½
Anchor Mills. E. W. Scarborough Co	.13
Angora. Whiting Paper Co. 21x33—60. Ream	16.90
Antique Flax. M. Plummer & Co	.15
Antique Flax. Raynor & Perkins Envelope Co	N
Antique Flax Linen. Raynor & Perkins Env. Co.	N
* Antique Oak. Whiting Paper Co. 21x33-60. Ream,	20.00

1

ANTIQUE PARCHMENT. Alexander Pirie & Sons.. ...... $0.32
*APOLLO. Henry Lindenmeyr & Sons...................... .08½
ARCHIVE BOND. Miller, Sloan & Wright................ .16
ARCHIVE LINEN. Miller, Sloan & Wright................ .16
ARCHIVE LINEN LEDGER. Miller, Sloan & Wright... .15
ARDMORE BOND. Clement & Stockwell.................. .15
ARGYLE LINEN. Whiting Paper Co........................ .17
*ARION. E. J. Merriam................................ .06½
ASHMERE DECKLE EDGE. Union Card & Paper Co. .12
ASHMERE LEDGER. Union Card & Paper Co.......... .12
*ATLANTIC. M. Plummer & Co........................... .07½
ATLAS LINEN. J. G. Shaw Blank Book Co.............. N
ATLAS MILLS. Geo. H. Simpson & Co.................... .07
AUSTRALIAN MAIL. G. B. Hurd & Co. 22x34. Ream, 6.00
*AVON. J. H. Walker................................... .04½

B

BANK BOND. Union Card & Paper Co.................... .11
BANK EXCHANGE LINEN. Geo. H. Simpson & Co.... .15
BANK LINEN. Melvin T. Hard.......................... .15
BANK NOTE BOND. Geo. B. Hurd & Co. 17x22—20.
    Ream 5.00
BANK RECORD LEDGER. J. F. Sarle..................... .15
BANKER'S BOND. Vernon Bros. & Co.................... .11½
BANKER'S LEDGER. Molleson Bros. Co.................. .13
BANKER'S LINEN. E. J. Merriam........................ .20
BANKER'S PARCHMENT. T. W. Paper. Raynor &
    Perkins Envelope Co.................................. N
BAY STATE. Phœnix Card & Paper Co................ .08
BEECHWOOD LINEN. C. T. Bainbridge & Sons......... .15
BEEKMAN MILLS. Melvin T. Hard...................... .17
BERKELEY LEDGER. Conrow Bros....................... .14
BERLIN LINEN. M. Plummer & Co...................... .08½
BERLIN MILLS. Berlin & Jones Envelope Co.......... .10
*BEST LINEN. H. Lindenmeyr & Sons.................... .16
BIRCH BARK. Geo. B. Hurd & Co. 21x33. Ream, 18.75
*BIRCHWOOD. Whiting Paper Co. 21x33-60. Ream, 24.50
BIRD'S EYE LINEN. Geo. B. Hurd & Co................ N

' BIRD'S EYE MAPLE. Geo. B. Hurd & Co. 20½x33.
Ream... $25.00
' BLEEKER LEDGER. H. Lindenmeyr & Sons............. .09
' BLINDMAN'S. Geo. B. Hurd & Co. 17x22. Ream... 9.50
' BLUE WOVE. J. E. Linde Paper Co....................... .11
' BLUE WOVE. F. A. Flinn................................ .10½
BRADFORD MILLS. Conrow Bros........................... .07
' BRAXTON. Miller, Sloan & Wright...................... .05½
' BREVOORT. Miller, Sloan & Wright..................... .08½
' BRENTWOOD. Miller, Sloan & Wright.................... .10
BRENTWOOD LIN. LED. Liebenroth, Von Auw & Co. N
BROADWAY. Tower Mfg. Co................................. N
BROKER'S LINEN. M. Plummer & Co..................... .18
BROOKDALE BOND. H. Lindenmeyr & Sons............ .11
BROWN'S ALL LINEN. All dealers.......................... List
' BROWN'S HAND MADE. Miller, Sloan & Wright...... List
BROWN'S LINEN LEDGER. All dealers...................... List
BRUNSWICK LINEN. Whiting Paper Co.................. .14
BRUNSWICK LINEN LEDGER. J. E. Linde Paper Co... .13
BULLION BOND. Miller, Sloan & Wright.................. .10
BURMESE IVORY. Geo. B. Hurd & Co. 21x33—60.
Ream... 12.00
BYRON WESTON'S LEDGER. All dealers.................. List

C

CALDENO MILLS. Conrow Bros .... .10
* CAMBRIC. Whiting Paper Co. 21x33—60. Ream, 15.00
* CAMBRIDGE. Molleson Bros. Co.......................... .09
CAMBRIDGE LINEN. Geo. B. Hurd & Co. 21x33—42.
Ream... 7.56
CAMBRIDGE MILLS. Molleson Bros. Co....... .... .10
* CANVAS SUPERFINE. Geo. B. Hurd & Co. 21x33.
Ream... 21.00
CAPITOL LINEN LEDGER. J. E. Linde Paper Co....... .12
CAREW SUPERFINE. E. J. Merriam....................... .17
CAREW LINEN LEDGER. E. J. Merriam.................. .16
CAREW PEERLESS BOND. Molleson Bros. Co.......... .18
CASCADE. Junger Paper Co............................... .07½

3

B
C
D
E
F
G
H
I
J
K
L
M
N
O
P
Q
R
S
T
U
V
W
Y

CASTLEWOOD COVERS. Molleson Bros. Co............... $0.07½
CAXTON BOND. Molleson Bros. Co...................... .18
CENTURY. Whiting Paper Co............................. .11
CENTURY LINEN. J. F. Sarle........................... .15
CHAMPION MILLS. Molleson Bros. Co.................... .14
CHAUNCEY BOND. Whiting Pap. Co. No. 25. 21x33.
    Ream.. 7.20
* CHELSEA MILLS. F. A. Flinn........................... .07½
* CITY. Union Card & Paper Co.......................... .05
CLINTON BOND. R. C. Kastner.......................... .15
* COARSE LAID LINEAR. Geo. B. Hurd & Co. 21x33.
    Ream.. 15.00
* COLD. H. Lindenmeyr & Sons........................... .08
COLD SPRING. E. J. Merriam........................... .11
COLONIAL LINEN. Miller, Sloan & Wright............... .14
* COLORED WOVE. F. A. Flinn............................. .10½
COLUMBIA LINEN. Marcus Ward & Co. 21x33.
    Ream.. 10.80
COLUMBUS LINEN. F. A. Flinn........................... .15
* COMET. H. Lindenmeyr & Sons.......................... .05½
COMMERCIAL BOND. Conrow Bros...................... List
COMMERCIAL LEDGER. Conrow Bros.................... .15
* COMMERCIAL LINEN. Alexander Pirie & Sons........... .12
COMMERCIAL SAFETY. Miller, Sloan & Wright......... List
* CONGRESS. Whiting Paper Co. 21x33—60. Ream, 15.00
CONGRESS BOND. E. J. Merriam........................ .16
CONGRESS LINEN. Clement & Stockwell................ .13
CONQUEROR. E. J. Merriam............................. .08½
CONSULATE LINEN. Whiting Paper Co. 21x33—60.
    Ream.. 22.50
CONTINENTAL WOVE. Geo. B. Hurd & Co. 21x33
    —60. Ream... 12.00
CONTRACT BOND. J. F. Sarle........................... .11
* COQUILLE SUPERFINE. Geo. B. Hurd & Co. 21x33.
    Ream.. 21.00
CORONA LINEN. J. E. Linde Paper Co.................. .06
CORONET MILLS. J. E. Linde Paper Co................. .13
CORPORATION BOND. J. E. Linde Paper Co............. .12
COUNTING HOUSE LINEN. J. E. Linde Paper Co....... .16

4

COUPON BOND. J. F. Sarle.. $0.20
COURT VELLUM. Marcus Ward & Co. 21x33. Rm., 10.80
CRANE & CO.'s BONDS. All dealers........................ List
CRANE'S ALL LINEN. Geo. B. Hurd & Co. and J. F.
Anderson, Jr. & Co. Ream........................... List
CRANE'S BASKET. G. B. Hurd & Co. 21x33. Ream, 15.00
CRANE'S DOESKIN. Geo. B. Hurd & Co. 21x33—70.
Ream.. 20.00
CRANE'S ETCHING. Geo. B. Hurd & Co. 21x33—70.
Ream.. 23.75
CRANE'S EXTRA SUPERFINE. Geo. B. Hurd & Co.
21x33—50. Ream...................................... 15.63
CRANE'S GRECIAN ANTIQUE. Geo. B. Hurd & Co.
21x33—70. Ream...................................... 23.75
CRANE'S JAPANESE LINEN. All dealers.................... List
CRANE'S KID FINISH. Geo. B. Hurd & Co. 21x33
—80. Ream... 25.00
CRANE'S LANCIERS. G. B. Hurd & Co. 21x33. Ream, 15.00
CRANE'S OLD STYLE. Geo. B. Hurd & Co. 21x33
Ream.. 23.75
CRANE'S OLD STYLE BOND. Geo. B. Hurd & Co.
21x33. No. 25. Ream...... .... 26.50
CRANE S PARCHMENT VELLUM. Geo. B. Hurd & Co.
21x33—70. Ream...................................... 23.75
CRANE'S RECORD LEDGER. All dealers.................... List
CRANE'S SUPER. Geo. B. Hurd & Co. 21x33—50.
Ream.. 12.50
CRANE'S TWILLED FLAX. Geo. B. Hurd & Co.
21x33—54. Ream...................................... 15.00
* CRANFORD. E. J. Merriam.............................. .14
* CRASH. Whiting Paper Co. 21x33—60. Ream...... 15.00
* CREAM LAID ANTIQUE. Molleson Bros. Co.............. .11
* CREPE DE CHINE SUPERFINE. Geo. B. Hurd & Co.
21x33. Ream... 21.00
* CRESCENT. H. Lindenmeyr & Sons...................... .13½
CRESCENT MILLS. E. W. Scarborough Co.............. .09
* CRINOLINE. Whiting Paper Co. 21x33—60. Ream, 15.00
CRITERION LINEN. Geo. H. Simpson & Co.............. .08
CROWN LEGHORN LINEN. J. F. Anderson, Jr. & Co.. .16

5

D
E
F
G
H
I
J
K
L
M
N
O
P
Q
R
S
T
U
V
W
Y

CROWN ROYAL LINEN. Junger Paper Co................ $0.11
CUMBERLAND LINEN LEDGER. Molleson Bros. Co.... .16
CURRENCY LINEN. J. B. Watkins.................. .13

D

*DAMASK. Geo. B. Hurd & Co. 21x33. Ream........ 21.00
DAMASK LINENE. Standard Card & Paper Co......... .18
*DANA MILLS. R. C. Kastner.................................. .07
DANE'S AMOSKEAG LINEN. Wm. P. Dane............... .13½
DANE'S BEST LINEN. Wm. P. Dane........:............... .18
DANE'S EXTRA STRONG LINEN BOND. Wm. P. Dane. .22
DANE'S IMPERIAL BOSCAWEN LINEN. Wm. P. Dane.
    Light, Ream, $10.00. Heavy, Ream................ 15.00
DANE'S ROYAL AMSTERDAM LINEN. Wm. P. Dane.
    Ream.. 10.00
DANE'S WILTON BOND. Wm. P. Dane.................... .13½
DARTFORD LINEN. H. Lindenmeyr & Sons............. .14
DEERLAKE MILLS. Union Card & Paper Co........... .10½
DEFIANCE LEDGER. J. F. Anderson, Jr. & Co......... .18
DEFIANCE MILLS. E. W. Scarborough Co............... .06
DELEVAN LEDGER. Conrow Bros......................... .10
*DELAWARE MILLS. Molleson Bros. Co................... .09
*DELTA MILLS. Melvin T. Hard........................... .08½
*DELTA MILLS. Junger Paper Co......................... .11
*DIAMOND "C" LEDGER. Whiting Paper Co............. .10
*DIANA. H. Lindenmeyr & Sons........................... .08½
*DIPLOMATIQUE. Geo. B. Hurd & Co. 17x22. Ream, 9.00
DISTAFF LINEN. (Crane's.) Geo. B. Hurd & Co.
    21x33—42. Ream... 17.50
DOESKIN. Geo. B. Hurd & Co. 21x33—60. Ream, 17.50
*DOLPHIN. H. Lindenmeyr & Sons....................... .08½
DOVER LINEN LEDGER. J. F. Anderson, Jr. & Co..... .14
DRAGON BOND. H. Lindenmeyr & Sons................. .07
*DUAL WOVE. Whiting Paper Co. 21x33. Ream... 18.00
DUANE LEDGER. Miller, Sloan & Wright.............. .10
DUBLIN LINEN. Berlin & Jones Envelope Co........... .08
DUNDEE BOND. Vernon Bros. & Co....................... .15

6

DUNDEE RECORD LEDGER. Vernon Bros. & Co........ $0.17
*DUODESCENT. G. B. Hurd & Co. 21x33—60. Ream, 21.00
DYNAMO. J. B. Watkins.. .08

E

*EAGLE. J. H. Walker............................. .. .08½
EARLY ENGLISH. (Crane's.) Geo. B. Hurd & Co.
    21x33. Ream................................ 23.75
*EAST HARTFORD. Standard Card & Paper Co........ .18
EAU CLAIR. Standard Card & Paper Co................ .08
EBATHAM BOND. H. Lindenmeyr & Sons................ .17½
EDINBURGH LINEN. Whiting Paper Co. 21x33—54.
    Ream......................... 12.35
*EGGSHELL DRAWING. American News Co.............. N
EGYPTIAN LINEN. Geo. B. Hurd & Co. 17x22—20.
    Ream.................... 5.00
ELECTRIC LINEN. J. B. Watkins............................ .18
ELECTRIC LINEN LEDGER. J. B. Watkins................ .14
ELMORE LEDGER. Conrow Bros.................. .... .12
ELWOOD BOND. J. F. Anderson, Jr. & Co............... List
EMPIRE BOND. Geo. H. Simpson & Co................... .12
EMPIRE LINEN. J. F. Sarle................................. .12
ENGLISH CREAM LAID. Geo. B. Hurd & Co. 21x33.
    Ream 18.75
ENGLISH LINEN. Geo. B. Hurd & Co. Ream.......... 21.00
*ENGLISH REPP. Geo. B. Hurd & Co. 21x33. Ream, 21.00
ENGLISH VELLUM. Whiting Paper Co. 21x33—50.
    Ream ....,.. 9.00
ETCHING. Geo. B. Hurd & Co. 21x33—60. Ream, 18.75
*ETNA. Phœnix Card & Paper Co............. .10
*EUREKA. Phœnix Card & Paper Co....................... .11
*EXCELSIOR. Phœnix Card & Paper Co.................... .12½
EXCELSIOR SUPERFINE. Kiggins & Tooker Co......... N
EXCHANGE LINEN. Conrow Bros......................... .18
EXPOSITION BOND. Whiting Paper Co................... .14
EXPRESS BOND. J. H. Walker............................ .12½
*EXTRA FINE. M. Plummer & Co......................... .10

7

D
E
F
G
H
I
J
K
L
M
N
O
P
Q
R
S
T
U
V
W
Y

Extra Fine Linen Laid. G. B. Hurd & Co. 21x33
—54. Ream... $10.80
Extra Fine Linen Wove. G. B. Hurd & Co. 21x33
—60. Ream... 10.80
Extra Strong Blank Book. Conrow Bros.......... .11

F

* Favorite. Berlin & Jones Envelope Co................. .11
* Favorite. J. F. Sarle.............................. .12
* Fayette Mills. Conrow Bros........................... .07
Federal. Junger Paper Co............................. .12
Federal Bond. W. H. Hasbrouck & Co.............. S
* Fine White Wove. Whiting Paper Co. 21x33—40.
Ream... 7.50
Finest Quality Linen. P. H. Hake Mfg. Co......... N
* Fleur de Lis Super. Geo. B. Hurd & Co. 21x33.
Ream... 21.00
Foreign Mail. W. H. Hasbrouck & Co............... S
Forty-seven (47) Bond. F. A. Flinn.................... .12
Forty-seven, Eleven (47 11) Bond. F. A. Flinn.... List
Franklin Linen Ledger. R. C. Kastner.............. 12½
* French Crépon. Whiting Paper Co. 21x33—50.
Ream... 9.00
* French Folio. Conrow Bros. Ream.................. 3.50
Fulton Bond. Molleson Bros. Co....................... .08

G

* Gazelle. J. F. Sarle.............................. .12
Genuine Irish Linen. P. H. Hake Mfg. Co........... N
* Germania Mills. F. A. Flinn........................ .05
Glasgow Linen. E. W. Scarborough Co............... .18
Glazed Bond. W. H. Hasbrouck & Co.................. S
Glendale. Junger Paper Co........................... .09
Gleneida Mills. J. E. Linde Paper Co.............. .11
Glenhurst Mills. Union Card & Paper Co.......... .09
* Glenmore Linen. Miller, Sloan & Wright.............. .07
Globe Linen Ledger. Liebenroth, Von Auw & Co. N

8

GOLD BOND. F. A. Flinn................................ $0.10
GOLD BOND. M. Plummer & Co.......................... .09
GOLDEN FLEECE. W. H. Hasbrouck & Co............. S
*GOLF LAID. Whiting Paper Co. 21x33—60. Ream, 13.50
*GOLF LAID BOND. Whiting Paper Co. No. 25.
    21x33. Ream................................ 12.50
GOSHEN LINEN. Conrow Bros............................ .07½
*GOTHAM LAID. Geo. B. Hurd & Co. 21x33—60.
    Ream.. 12.00
GOVERNMENT BOND. Conrow Bros........................ .16
GOVERNMENT LINEN. J. F. Anderson, Jr. & Co......... .16
*GRAMERCY. Miller, Sloan & Wright................... .07
GRAMERCY MILLS. H. J. Bates......................... N
*GRAND QUADRILLE. Whiting Paper Co. 21x33.
    10 kilo. Ream.................................... 12.60
*GRANITE Whiting Paper Co. 21x33—50. Ream... 10.00
*GREATER NEW YORK. Geo. H. Simpson & Co......... .06
GRECIAN BOND. Whiting Paper Co. No. 25. 21x33.
    Ream... 12.50
GRECIAN PARCHMENT. W. H. Hasbrouck & Co....... S
GREYLOCK LINEN LEDGER. Miller, Sloan & Wright. .16
GROS GRAIN SUPERFINE. Geo. B. Hurd & Co. 21x33.
    Ream... 21.00
GUARANTY BOND. Miller, Sloan & Wright.............. .10

H

HAILSTONE SUPERFINE. J. B. Watkins.................. .08
HAKE'S CHAMOIS FINISH. P. H. Hake Mfg. Co....... N
*HAMILTON MILLS. American News Co.................... N
HAMPDON. M. Plummer & Co........................... .09½
*HAND MADE. G. B. Hurd & Co. 21x33—54. Ream, 16.20
*HAND MADE. Whiting Pap. Co. 21x33—60. Ream, 15.00
*HAND MADE PARCHMENT. G. B. Hurd & Co. 21x33
    —60. Ream....................................... 33.00
HAND MADE PARCHMENT. J. E. Linde Paper Co.
    22x34. Ream..................................... 13.00
HARRICON FLATS. F. A. Flinn.......................... .15
HARVARD LINEN. Junger Paper Co..................... .06½

9

F
G
H
I
J
K
L
M
N
O
P
Q
R
S
T
U
V
W
Y

HAWTHORNE MILLS LIN. LED.   G. H. Simpson & Co. $0.16
*HECLA.   H. Lindenmeyr & Sons.............................   .05
HERCULES LINEN.   E. J. Merriam.........................   .10
HIGH GRADE.   Tower Mfg. Co..........................   N
*HIGHLAND ANTIQUE.   G. B. Hurd & Co.   21x33—60.
    Ream..   15.00
*HIGHLAND HEATHER.   Geo. B. Hurd & Co.   21x33
    —60.   Ream...   21.88
HOCKANUM.   J. H. Walker..   .06
H. L. BOND.   H. Lindenmeyr & Sons.....................   .10½
HOLLAND LINEN.   H. J. Bates.............................   N
*HOME MADE.   M. Plummer & Co............................   .13
HOME RULE LINEN.   M. Plummer & Co..................   .12
HONEST LINEN.   Union Card & Paper Co...............   .07
HORICON.   F. A. Flinn..   .15
*HOWARD MILLS.   F. A. Flinn.................................   .08½
HUDSON MILLS.   J. E. Linde Paper Co.....................   .07½
HURD'S IRISH LINEN.   Geo. B. Hurd & Co.   21x33
    —54.   Ream...   10.80
HYPERION LINEN.   E. J. Merriam..........................   .06½
*HYPERION LINEN LEDGER.   Miller, Sloan & Wright...   .14

I

*IMITATION CORK.   Geo. B. Hurd & Co.   20½x33.
    Ream...   25.00
IMPERIAL.   E. J. Merriam......................................   .12
IMPERIAL BOND.   Whiting Paper Co.   No. 21.   21x33.
    Ream...   8.00
IMPERIAL CROWN.   P. H. Hake Mfg. Co.................   N
IMPERIAL IRISH LINEN.   Raynor & Perkins Env. Co.   List
IMPERIAL LEDGER.   Geo. B. Hurd & Co.   21x33
    —60.   Ream...   18.75
INDENTURE BOND.   Melvin T. Hard.........................   .11½
INDIA PROOF.   Whiting Paper Co.   21x33—60. Rm.,   22.50
INDIA LINEN.   Standard Card & Paper Co...............   .08
INDIA MAIL.   Geo. B. Hurd & Co.   22x34.   Ream...   6.00
INSURANCE SPECIAL.   (J. B. W.)   J. B. Watkins.........   .09
IRISH LINEN.   Whiting Paper Co.   21x33—54. Rm.,   10.80

10

IRISH LINEN. Geo. B. Hurd & Co. 21x33—54. Rm., $10.80
IROQUOIS BOND. Molleson Bros. Co......................... .15
IROQUOIS LINEN. Molleson Bros. Co........................ .15
* ISLAND CITY MILLS. American News Co............... N
ITASCA BOND. Standard Card & Paper Co.............. .12

J

JAPAN BOND. Geo. B. Hurd & Co. 17x22—20.
Ream.. 5.00
JAPAN PARCHMENT. Geo. B. Hurd & Co. 17x22
—20. Ream... 17.50
JAPANESE. Whiting Paper Co. 21x33—60. Ream, 22.50
JAPANESE LINEN. (Crane's). All dealers.................. List
JEFFERSON. F. A. Flinn... .08
JUDICIAL BOND. Conrow Bros................................ .11
* JUNO LINEN. H. Lindenmeyr & Sons..................... .10
* JUPITER. H. Lindenmeyr & Sons........................... .08
* JUPITER LINEN. H. Lindenmeyr & Sons.................. 06½

K

KEITH'S LEDGER. H. Lindenmeyr & Sons............... List
* KENNEBEC MILLS. Standard Card & Paper Co....... .07
KING BOND. A. B. King & Co............................... .16
KINGSTON MILLS. H. J. Bates............................. N
KNICKERBOCKER LEDGER. Molleson Bros. Co.......... .11

L

* "L" in a diamond. H. Lindenmeyr & Sons........... .08
* "L" in a diamond. Whiting Paper Co.................. .10
LAFAYETTE LEDGER. J. F. Sarle...................... .13
LAKE CITY. J. F. Sarle.................................... .11
* LA MONTE QUADRILLE. Geo. B. Hurd & Co. 17x22
—8 kilo. Ream.. 4.48
LARCHMONT. J. G. Shaw Blank Book Co.............. N
* LAUREL. H. Lindenmeyr & Sons......................... .13½
* LA VOGUE. Whiting Paper Co........................... .13
LENOX BOND. Molleson Bros. Co....................... .13

11

I
J
K
L
M
N
O
P
Q
R
S
T
U
V
W
Y

* LEVANT PARCHMENT. Geo. B. Hurd & Co. 21x33
—60. Ream.. $10.80
LEXINGTON. Raynor & Perkins Envelope Co............ N
LINCOLN MILLS. Raynor & Perkins Envelope Co..... N
* LINDEN. H. Lindenmeyr & Sons............................. .10½
LINDHURST MILLS. J. E. Linde Paper Co............... .09½
* LINEN CLOTH. Whiting Paper Co. 21x33—60.
Ream... 22.50
* LINEN CLOTH SUPER. Geo. B. Hurd & Co. 21x33.
Ream 21.00
* LINEN FABRIC. Whiting Paper Co. 17x22—20....... .19
* LINEN FLOSS BOND. Marcus Ward & Co. 21x33.
Ream... 7.20
LINEN LEDGER. Whiting Paper Co........................ .20
LINEN LEDGER. M. Plummer & Co. .... .08
* LINEN QUADRILLE. Geo. B. Hurd & Co. 17x22.
Ream 6.00
L. L. BROWN'S LEDGER. All dealers....................... List
L. L. BROWN PAPER CO., FINE. All dealers............ List
LONDON MILLS. Whiting Paper Co....................... .08
LONGFELLOW LINEN. Whiting Paper Co. 21x33
—54. Ream.. 12.00
* LORANE. M. Plummer & Co............................... .07

M

MADE IN AMERICA (Bonds and Ledgers). J. B.
Watkins... .20
MAGNA CHARTA BOND. J. F. Anderson, Jr. & Co.... .20
MAGNET MILLS. Union Card & Paper Co.............. .06
* MAGNET MILLS. Standard Card & Paper Co.......... .06½
MALTESE COLORED FLATS. Miller, Sloan & Wright. .12
MALTESE LINEN. Miller, Sloan & Wright............... .13
MALTESE LINEN. J. E. Linde Paper Co.................. .12
* MANHATTAN. F. A. Flinn................................. .11½
* MAPLEWOOD. Whiting Paper Co. 21x33—60. Rm., 24.50
* MARCUS WARD & CO.'S EVERY DAY. 21x33—50.
Ream 7.50
* MARCUS WARD & CO.'S FLEUR DE LYS, FINE. 21x33, .16

12

*Mascot. M. Plummer & Co.............................. $0.06½
Matchless Linen. P. H. Hake Mfg. Co............. N
* Mazy. P. H. Hake Mfg. Co................................ N
Mercantile Bond. H. Lindenmeyr & Sons.......... 17½
Mercantile Linen. C. W. Williams & Co............. .13
Merchants' Linen Ledger. Vernon Bros. & Co.... .10
* Middlesex Mills. Molleson Bros. Co.................. .07½
* Midwood. E. J. Merriam.............................. .07½
Milan Linen Ledger. J. F. Anderson, Jr. & Co..... .11
* Mill 8 Bond. Conrow Bros.............................. .17
* Mill 9. J. E. Linde Paper Co............................ .06
* Mill 14. Conrow Bros...................................... .11
* Mill 22. Conrow Bros...................................... .05
* Mill 24. J. E. Linde Paper Co......................... .05
* Mill 39. Vernon Bros. & Co............................. .06
* Mill 45. J. E. Linde Paper Co.......................... .07½
* Mill 50. J. E. Linde Paper Co......................... .04½
* Mill 87. Vernon Bros. & Co............................. .04½
Minerva Bond. H. Lindenmeyr & Sons................ .14½
* Minerva Ledger. H. Lindenmeyr & Sons............. .14½
Minerva Linen. Clement & Stockwell.................. .08½   M
Mohican Linen. F. A. Flinn and Miller, Sloan &
    Wright.. .10   N
* Moire Poplin Gray. Geo. B. Hurd & Co. 21x33.   O
    Ream.. 21.00
* Momie Cloth. Whiting Paper Co. 21x33—60.   P
    Ream... 15.00
Monarch Bond. Marcus Ward & Co. 21x33. Rm., 9.00   Q
Monarch Linen. J. E. Linde Paper Co................. .15
* Monarch Mills. C. W. Williams & Co................. .09   R
* Monogram. M. Plummer & Co........................... .12
* Monogram Laid. M. Plummer & Co.................... .12   S
Monogram Linen. Whiting Paper Co. 22x34—54.
    Ream... 10.80   T
Monroe Ledger. E. W. Scarborough Co.............. .14
*Montauk. J. F. Anderson, Jr. & Co...................... .16   U
Montauk Linen. Molleson Bros. Co..................... .10
Montauk Linen Ledger. J. E. Linde Paper Co..... .09   V
Montauk Mills. J. F. Anderson, Jr. & Co............ .17   W

13
                                                                         Y

MONTROS LINEN. Miller, Sloan & Wright................ $0.10
MORRIS. Tower Mfg. Co................................... N
MOTTLED VELLUM. Berlin & Jones Envelope Co..... N
*M., S. & W. SPECIAL. Miller, Sloan & Wright.. ..... .09
*MT. HOPE MILLS. Melvin T. Hard...................... .10

N

NAPIER BOND. Melvin T. Hard............................. .12½
NAPLES LINEN. H. Lindenmeyr & Sons................. .16
NASSAU BOND. Molleson Bros. Co...................... .13
*NATIONAL. Vernon Bros. & Co.......................... .11
NATIONAL BANK LIN. LEDG. Geo. H. Simpson & Co. .11
NATIONAL LINEN, (Eagle). E. W. Scarborough Co. .14
NATIONAL LINEN. J. E. Linde Paper Co.............. .12
NATIONAL SAFETY, (La Monte's). All dealers........ List
NEAPOLITAN BOND. Berlin & Jones Envelope Co...... N
NEMO LEDGER. Melvin T. Hard........................... .12
*NEPTUNE. H. Lindenmeyr & Sons....................... .06½
NEW ENGLAND MILLS. J. F. Sarle....................... .12
NEW FLAX. W. H. Hasbrouck & Co..................... S
NEW YORK STANDARD LINEN. Vernon Bros. & Co... .10
*No. 1 BLUE WOVE. Molleson Bros. Co................ .11
*No. 1 COLORED LAID. All dealers...................... .11
*No. 1 EXTRA QUALITY. Whiting Paper Co. 21x33
    —60. Ream... 16.90
*No. 1 QUALITY. Whiting Paper Co. 21x33—60.
    Ream 13.50
*No. 1 TINTED WOVE, (Parsons). All dealers........... .11
No. 1 WOVE TINT. Vernon Bros. & Co.................. .10
*No. 2 COLORED LAID. All dealers....................... .07
*No. 2 LEDGER. J. E. Linde Paper Co.................. .12
*No. 2 LEDGER. M. Plummer & Co...................... .12½
*No. 2 LEDGER. Melvin T. Hard.......................... .14
*No. 3 LEDGER. Melvin T. Hard.......................... .12
*No. 4 LEDGER. Melvin T. Hard......... .... .10½
No. 4 WHITE WOVE. Whiting Paper Co................ .08
*No. 12 LEDGER. H. Lindenmeyr & Sons................ .12½
*No. 38 SPECIAL. R. C. Kastner........................... .08½

*No. 80 White Wove. Miller, Sloan & Wright........ $0.06
*No. 87 White. Vernon Bros. & Co........................ .05½
*No. 121 Bond. M. Plummer & Co.................. ...... .17
*Nonpareil. J. F. Sarle............................... .08½
* Non-Transparent Bond. G. B. Hurd & Co. 22x34.
    Ream... 17.50
*North River. Vernon Bros. & Co........................ ... .07½
Norwood Mills. J. E. Linde Paper Co.................. .08½
*N. Y. Wove. Whiting Paper Co............................. .10

O

Oakland Linen. J. F. Sarle..... .... .10
Oakleaf Linen. J. F. Anderson, Jr. & Co.............. .10
*Oak Mills. Molleson Bros. Co............................ .07
Oakwood Mills. Union Card & Paper Co............ .06½
Odin. Liebenroth, Von Auw & Co......................... N
Official Bond. R. C. Kastner............................ .14
Official Linen. R. C. Kastner........................... .12½
Old Berkshire. Geo. B. Hurd & Co. 21x33—50.
    Ream 10.00
Old Berkshire Mills. Melvin T. Hard................ .16
Old Crown Linen. Union Card & Paper Co.......... .10
*Old Dominion. M. Plummer & Co......................... .15
Old English. J. E. Linde Paper Co....................... .16
Old English Bond. Conrow Bros...................... .15
Old English Linen. Conrow Bros...................... .15
Old Fashioned Linen. Berlin & Jones Envelope Co. .15
Old Fashioned Linen. Wm. P. Dane. Ream......... 7.00
Old Flax Linen. W. H. Hasbrouck & Co.............. S
Old Flax Parchment. W. H. Hasbrouck & Co..... S
Old Hampden. H. Lindenmeyr & Sons, M. Plummer
    & Co. and Conrow Bros.................................... .17
Old Hampshire Bond. E. J. Merriam................... .18
Old Hempstead Bond. J. F. Sarle.................... .14
Old Holland Linen. W. H. Hasbrouck & Co........ N
Old Style Vellum. C. T. Bainbridge & Sons........ .20
Old Vermont Bond. Union Card & Paper Co...... .13
Olympia Bond. C. W. Williams & Co................... .10

N
O
P
Q
R
S
T
U
V
W
Y

OLYMPIA LINEN. C. W. Williams & Co................... $0.09
*ONION SKIN. J. E. Linde Paper Co. Ream............. 3.00
*ONION SKIN. Whiting Paper Co. 17x22. Ream..... 5.50
*ONION SKIN QUADRILLE. Whiting Paper Co. 17x22.
    Ream.................. 5.50
*ORIENT MAIL. Whiting Paper Co. 21x33. Ream, 13.50
*ORIENTAL LINEN. J. E. Linde Paper Co................. .11
*ORIGINAL CULTER MILLS. G. B. Hurd & Co. 21x33.
    Ream.................. 12.50
*ORIGINAL TURKEY LINEN. Whiting Paper Co. 22x34
    —54. Ream.................. 16.20
*OTSEGO. Standard Card & Paper Co.................... .12
*OUR FAVORITE. J. F. Sarle..................... .10
*OUR NEW LINEN. Tower Mfg. Co......................... N
*OUR SPECIAL. Whiting Paper Co........................ .09
*OVERLAND. Whiting Paper Co. 17x22. Ream...... 4.50
*OVERLAND MAIL. G. B. Hurd & Co. 17x22. Ream, 5.25
*OVERLAND MAIL. Marcus Ward & Co. 21x33. Rm., 7.00

P

*PALISADES. Vernon Bros. & Co. Folded........ .... .08
PARAGON LINEN. (W., S. & B.) Wyckoff, Seamans
    & Benedict. 17x22—16. Ream..................... 8.40
PARCHMENT. Whiting Pap. Co. 21x33—54. Ream, 21.35
PARCHMENT BOND. J. E. Linde Paper Co............... .16
PARCHMENT VELLUM. Raynor & Perkins Env. Co... N
PARSONS BOND. H. Lindenmeyr & Sons................. List
PARSONS EX. SUPERFINE. Conrow Bros................. .14
PARSONS TINTED WRITINGS. All Dealers............ ...... .11
*PATRIOT LINEN LEDGER. C. W. Williams & Co........ .12
*PEBBLE (SUPER.) G. B. Hurd & Co. 21x33. Ream, 21.00
PEERLESS LINEN. Raynor & Perkins Envelope Co. .14$\frac{2}{5}$
PEERLESS RECORD. W. H. Hasbrouck & Co............. S
PELHAM. J. G. Shaw Blank Book Co.................... N
*PEMBERTON MILLS. E. W. Scarborough Co........... .10
PEMBROOK LEDGER. F. A. Flinn and Miller, Sloan &
    Wright.................. .16
PENELOPE LINEN. J. E. Linde Paper Co.............. .09$\frac{1}{2}$
PEOPLE'S LINEN. Conrow Bros......................... .10

PERFECTION IRISH LINEN. Whiting Pap. Co. 21x33
—50. Ream... $9.00
PERSIAN BOND. Miller, Sloan & Wright................ .12
PHŒNIX. Phœnix Card & Paper Co..................... .07
PIONEER LEDGER. J. F. Anderson, Jr. & Co........... .13
*PIQUET SUPERFINE. Geo. B. Hurd & Co. 21x33.
Ream.. .... 21.00
*PLAIN LEDGER. J. F. Sarle........... .... .09
POMPEIIAN. Whiting Pap. Co. 21x33—60. Ream, 22.50
PONTIAC LINEN. Molleson Bros. Co.................... .08
POPELINE. Whiting Paper Co. 21x33—60. Ream, 22.50
PORTSMOUTH. R. C. Kastner.............................. .12
POSTAL LEDGER. F. A. Flinn............................. .10
*POTOMAC LAID LINEN. F. A. Flinn................... .07½
PREMIER LINEN BOND. J. G. Shaw Blank Book Co. N
PREMIER LINEN LEDGER. J. G. Shaw Blank Book Co. N
PREMIER LINEN RECORD. J. G. Shaw Blank Book Co. N
PREMIUM BOND. C. W. Williams & Co.................. .16
PREMIUM LINEN. C. W. Williams & Co................... .18
PREMIUM LINEN LEDGER. C. W. Williams & Co...... .16
PRISTINE LINEN. F. A. Flinn............................. .12
PROGRESS. Liebenroth, Von Auw & Co................. N
PURE FLAX LINEN. Marcus Ward & Co. 21x33.
Ream.. 16.80
PURE IRISH LINEN. Raynor & Perkins Env. Co....... List
PURE LINEN. Whiting Paper Co.................. ..... .11½   P
PURE LINEN BOND. Berlin & Jones Envelope Co....... .20
PURE LINEN FABRIC. Geo. H. Simpson & Co.......... .10   Q
PURE LINEN STOCK. J. F. Anderson, Jr. & Co......... .18
PURE MONARCH LINEN. J. E. Linde Paper Co......... .15   R
PURITAN LEDGER. E. J. Merriam........................ .10   S
PURITAN LINEN. Syndicate Trading Co.................. S
*PURITAN MILLS. Raynor & Perkins Envelope Co..... N   T

Q

U

V

QUADRILLE. Geo. B. Hurd & Co. 17x22. Ream..... 6.00   W
QUADRILLE BOND. C. T. Bainbridge & Sons............ .25
17   Y

R

R & P. Raynor & Perkins Envelope Co................ N
RAVELSTONE. H. Lindenmeyr & Sons................ $0.16
RAVENSWOOD. F. A. Flinn............................. .10
*READE MILLS. Vernon Bros. & Co................... .07
*REAL INDIA IVORY. Geo. B. Hurd & Co. 21x33.
    Ream... 15.00
REAL IRISH LINEN. P. H. Hake Mfg. Co............. N
RECORD. Miller, Sloan & Wright.................... .11
RECORD BOND. J. E. Linde Paper Co................. .08½
RECORD LEDGER. M. Plummer & Co.................. .11
*RECORD LEDGER. Whiting Paper Co................. .11½
REDFERN. Liebenroth, Von Auw & Co............... N
REGENT LINEN, (W., S. & B.) Wyckoff, Seamans &
    Benedict. 17x22—16. Ream...................... 5.60
REGIMENTAL GRAY. Geo. B. Hurd & Co. 21x33—64.
    Ream... 29.35
*REPP. Whiting Paper Co. 21x33—60. Ream........ 22.50
REPP BOND No. 21. Whiting Paper Co. 21x33.
    Ream.. 22.00
RIVAL BOND. J. E. Linde Paper Co................. .08½
*RIVERDALE. M. Plummer & Co...................... .08
ROLLING STONE. E. W. Scarborough Co............. .06
ROMA. Liebenroth, Von Auw & Co................... N
ROMAN BOND. Miller, Sloan & Wright.............. .14
ROYAL ACADEMY. Marcus Ward & Co............... N
ROYAL BLUE. Geo. B. Hurd & Co. Ream............ 23.75
ROYAL BOND. Conrow Bros........................... List
ROYAL BROWN. Geo. B. Hurd & Co. Ream.......... 23.75
ROYAL CREAM. Geo.B. Hurd & Co. 21x33. Ream, 23.75
ROYAL ENGLISH LINEN. W. H. Hasbrouck & Co...... S
ROYAL ENGLISH VELLUM. W. H. Hasbrouck & Co... S
*ROYAL FROSTED VELLUM. Geo. B. Hurd & Co. 21x
    33—60. Ream.................................... 12.50
ROYAL GRAY. Geo. B. Hurd & Co. 21x33. Ream, 23.75
ROYAL INDIA IVORY. Marcus Ward & Co. 21x33.
    Ream... 21.60

*Royal Irish Linen. Marcus Ward & Co. 21x33
   —54. Ream... $21.60
Royal Irish Linen, Vellum Finish. Marcus Ward
   & Co. Ream.. 21.60
Royal Ledger. J. F. Anderson, Jr. & Co............. .17
*Royal Linen. Whiting Paper Co. 21x33—50.
   Ream.. 7.50
Royal Linen Ledger. J. F. Anderson, Jr. & Co...... .17
*Royal Princess. Raynor & Perkins Envelope Co.... N
Royal Purple. Geo. B. Hurd & Co. 21x33. Rm., 21.88
Royal Red. Geo. B. Hurd & Co. 21x33. Ream... 45.00
Royal Satin. Whiting Pap. Co. 21x32—60. Rm., 9.00
Royal Standard Plate. P. H. Hake Mfg. Co......... N
Royal Vellum. Geo. B. Hurd & Co. 21x33—60.
   Ream.. 15.00
*Royal Velvet. Whiting Paper Co. 21x33—60.
   Ream.. 9.00
Royal White. Geo. B. Hurd & Co. 21x33—60.
   Ream.. 18.75
Russian Blue. Geo. B. Hurd & Co. 21x33. Ream, 21.88
*Russian Leather Superfine. Geo. B. Hurd & Co.
   21x33. Ream... 21.00
Russian Linen Ledger. J. E. Linde Paper Co......... .16

S

*Sales 8 Bond. Conrow Bros................................... .17
*Sales 14. Conrow Bros.. .11
*Sales 22. Conrow Bros.. .05
*Sales 35. Melvin T. Hard..................................... .09½
*Sales 55. Melvin T. Hard...................................... .11
*Salmon River Mills. Melvin T. Hard................... 14
Saranac Linen. Union Card & Paper Co............... .13
Satin Wove. Geo. B. Hurd & Co. 21x33—50.
   Ream.. 10.00
*Saturn. H. Lindenmeyr & Sons............................. .07¾
Savoy Linen. E. W. Scarborough Co...................... .08
Saxon Linen Ledger. F. A. Flinn............................. .15

SCOTCH GRANITE. Geo. B. Hurd & Co. 21x33—50.
Ream... $10.00
SCOTCH LINEN LEDGER. All dealers. Up to 19x24, .20
Over 19x24.. .22
SECURITY TRUST BOND. Union Card & Paper Co...... .11½
SENATE BOND. Raynor & Perkins Envelope Co......... .16
*SENECA MILLS. Molleson Bros. Co............................. .12
SERVIA LINEN LEDGER. Miller, Sloan & Wright....... .12½
SEVENTY-ONE (71) BOND. F. A. Flinn...................... .16
SHAMROCK LINEN. American News Co..................... N
*SILVER WEDDING. Whiting Paper Co. 21x33—60.
Ream... 30.00
*SNOWFLAKE. Geo. B. Hurd & Co. 21x33. Ream... 18.75
*SNOWFLAKE. J. H. Walker...................................... .06
SOVEREIGN BOND. H. J. Bates .... N
SOVEREIGN LINEN. H. J. Bates............................... N
*SPECIAL. Whiting Paper Co...................................... .09
*SPECIAL LINEN CLOTH. Whiting Paper Co. 21x33
—60. Ream.. 15.00
*SPECIAL REPP. Whiting Paper Co. 21x33—60.
Ream... 15.00
SPRINGDALE SUPERFINE. F. A. Flinn...................... .13
SPRING LAKE MILLS. Geo. H. Simpson & Co.......... .11
SPRUCE MILLS. Geo. H. Simpson & Co.................... .09
SPRUCE MILLS BLUE WOVE No. 1. Geo. H. Simpson
& Co... .10
SPRUCE MILLS COLORED LAID No. 1. Geo. H. Simp-
son & Co.. .10
SPRUCE MILLS TINTED WOVE No. 1. Geo. H. Simp-
son & Co.. .10
*STAFF LINEAR. Geo. B. Hurd & Co. 21x33. Rm., 15.00
STANDARD BOND. Molleson Bros. Co...................... .11
*STANDARD LAID. Geo. B. Hurd & Co. 21x33—60.
Ream... 10.80
STANDARD LINEN. Whiting Paper Co. 21x33—54.
Ream... 18.65
STANDARD LINEN. Berlin & Jones Envelope Co......... .16
STANDARD LINEN LEDGER. Whiting Paper Co.......... .20
*STANDARD WOVE. Geo. B. Hurd & Co. 21x33—50.
Ream... 9.00

STAR LINEN. F. Flinn and Miller, Sloan & Wright. $0.17
STATE BOND. Whiting Paper Co............................ .17
STATE MILLS. J. E. Linde Paper Co................ .... .07
*ST. ELMO. Miller, Sloan & Wright........................ .09
*STELLA. H. Lindenmeyr & Sons............................ .08½
STERLING BOND. Clement & Stockwell.................... .20
STERLING LEDGER. Clement & Stockwell................ .15
STERLING LEDGER. Whiting Paper Co.................... .14
STERLING LINEN. Clement & Stockwell.................. .18
STEWART. Junger Paper Co.................................... .10½
STOCKBRIDGE LINEN. Phœnix Card & Paper Co...... .15
STONYWOOD LINEN. Alexander Pirie & Sons............ .16
*STRATFORD. Miller, Sloan & Wright...................... .06½
STRATHMORE DECKLE EDGE. Miller, Sloan & Wright. .20
STRATHMORE PARCHMENT. J. E. Linde Paper Co..... .20
SUPERFINE. Whiting Paper Co.............................. .16
SUPERFINE BOND. Junger Paper Co....................... .13
SUPER. TINTS (Laid and Wove). Whiting Paper Co. .10
*SUPERIOR. J. H. Walker.................................... .09½
SWAN BOND. Syndicate Trading Co....................... N
SWAN SATIN. Syndicate Trading Co........,............. N
SWAN VELLUM. Syndicate Trading Co.................... N
SYNDICATE BOND. R. C. Kastner......................... .10

T

TACONIC. Junger Paper Co.................................... .11
TEXTILE BOND. Whiting Paper Co........................ .09
TOKIO LINEN. Molleson Bros. Co.......................... .13
TORCHON. C. T. Bainbridge & Sons...................... .20
*TORCHON LINEN. Geo. B. Hurd & Co. 21x33—60.
  Ream.. 18.75
TRADE BOND. Whiting Paper Co.......................... .09
TRADE LINEN. Whiting Paper Co.......................... .09
TRADESMAN'S LINEN. H. Lindenmeyr & Sons........... 13½
TRADESMAN'S LEDGER. H. Lindenmeyr & Sons........ 13½
*TRANS-ATLANTIC. M. Ward & Co. 21x33. Ream, 7.00
TREASURY LINEN. Vernon Bros. & Co.................... .08½
TREMONT LINEN. Melvin T. Hard........................ .11

T
U
V
W
Y

TRILBY LINEN. Vernon Bros. & Co........................ $0.06½
TUNIS BOND. J. F. Anderson, Jr. & Co... .... .15

U

*UMBRIA. E. J. Merriam.. .09
UNION BOND. E. J. Merriam............ .... .12
UNITED STATES BOND. C. W. Williams & Co........... .13
UNITED STATES MILLS. Vernon Bros. & Co............. .11½
UNIVERSAL BOND. Vernon Bros. & Co..................... .14
UNIVERSITY LINEN. Vernon Bros. & Co................... .16
U. S. BOND. M. Plummer & Co............................... .13
U. S. LINEN BOND. Miller, Sloan & Wright............. .18
U. S. LINEN LAID AND WOVE. Miller, Sloan &
Wright.. .18
U. S. STANDARD LINEN. Raynor & Perkins Env. Co. .10

V

VALENCIA LINEN. J. E. Linde Paper Co................... .07½
VAN GELDER ZONEN'S HAND MADE. Miller, Sloan
& Wright... N
VELVET FINISH. P. H. Hake Mfg. Co..................... N
*VELVET FINISH PARCHMENT. Geo. B. Hurd & Co.
21x33—60. Ream...................................... 12.50
VELVETEEN. Berlin & Jones Envelope Co. 21x33
—80.. 10.80
*VENETIAN REPP SUPERFINE. Geo. B. Hurd & Co.
21x33. Ream.. 21.00
*VESTA. H. Lindenmeyr & Sons............................ .09
VESTA LINEN LEDGER. Liebenroth, Von Auw & Co. N
VICTOR MILLS. Standard Card & Paper Co............. .10
VICTORIA BOND. J. F. Anderson, Jr. & Co.............. .10
VICTORY BOND. Geo. H. Simpson & Co.................. .11
VIKING LINEN. H. Lindenmeyr & Sons.................. .07
VULCAN BOND. J. F. Sarle................................... .14
VULCAN LINEN. J. F. Sarle................................... .14

W

*WATERED SUPERFINE. Geo. B. Hurd & Co. 21x33. Ream..	$21.00
WATKINS, (Made in America.) J. B. Watkins...........	S
*WAVE SUPERFINE. Geo. B. Hurd & Co. 21x33. Ream..	21.00
WESTLOCK. H. Lindenmeyr & Sons......................	.14
WESTMINSTER VELLUM. Whiting Paper Co. 21x33 —50. Ream...	14.00
WESTON'S LINEN LEDGER. All dealers.....................	List
WEST POINT BLUE. Whiting Paper Co. 21x33—60. Ream...	12.00
*WEXFORD. Miller, Sloan & Wright.........................	.08
*WHITE LAID. Molleson Bros. Co..........................	.12
WHITING'S BOND No. 21. Whiting Paper Co. 21x 23. Ream..	16.20
WHITING'S LINEN FABRIC. Whiting Paper Co. 17x 22—20. Ream...	5.40
WHITING'S LINEN LEDGER. Whiting Paper Co. 17 x22—24. Ream..	6.50
WHITING'S SUPERFINE. Whiting Paper Co...............	.15
*WICHER. Geo. B. Hurd & Co. 21x33. Ream........	15.00
WILTON BOND. W. P. Dane.................................	.15
*WINSOR. M. Plummer & Co.................................	.11½
WINTHROP LINEN LEDGER. F. A. Flinn and Miller, Sloan & Wright...	.13
WORNOCK MILLS. Conrow Bros.............................	.08
WORONOCO BOND. J. F. Sarle...............................	.21
WORONOCO LEDGER. J. F. Sarle...........................	.20
WOVEN LINE. Whiting Paper Co. 21x33—60. Rm.,	22.50
W., S. & B. PARAGON. Wyckoff, Seamans & Benedict. 17x22—16. Ream.................................	8.40
W., S. & B. REGENT. Wyckoff, Seamans & Benedict. 17x22—16. Ream.................................	5.60
W., S. & B. REMINGTON. Wyckoff, Seamans & Benedict. 17x22—20. Ream...............................	5.60
W., S. & B. SUPERIOR LINEN. Wyckoff, Seamans & Benedict. 17x22. Ream.................................	3.00

Y

YE OLDE HOMESPUN. Geo. B. Hurd & Co. 21x33
—42. Ream... $9.45
*YORK MILLS. Whiting Paper Co.......................... .12

PRICE LIST OF AGAWAM PAPER CO.'S "AGAWAM BOND,"

WHITE AND TINTED. (Tinted in No. 21 only).

SIZES, THICKNESS AND PRICES PER 1,000 SHEETS.

Sizes.	15 x 19	16 x 21	17 x 22	17 x 28	19 x 24	19 x 30	22 x 34
"Agawam Bond," Thickness No. 21..	$6.25	$7.50	$8.00	$10.50	$10.00	$12.50	$16.00
" " " 25..	7.50	9.00	10.00	12.50	12.00	15.00	20.00
" " " 29..	8.75	11.00	11.50	14.50	14.00	17.50	23.00

Discount—30 per cent. full ream lots.
20 per cent. broken ream lots.

25

BROWN'S "ALL LINEN."

Price Per 500 Sheets.   Discount 35 Per Cent.

16 x 21,	6½-lb	$3.75	17 x 22,	14-lb	$6.25
"	8-lb	4.00	"	16-lb	6.75
"	10-lb	5.00	"	18-lb	7.25
"	12-lb	5.50	"	20-lb	8.00
"	14-lb	5.75	"	24-lb	9.60
"	16-lb	6.50	18 x 23,	14-lb	7.00
"	18-lb	7.25	"	16-lb	7.25
"	20-lb	8.00	"	18-lb	7.50
16 x 26,	8-lb	4.75	"	20-lb	8.00
"	10-lb	5.00	"	22-lb	8.80
"	12-lb	6.00	19 x 24,	14-lb	7.00
"	14-lb	7.00	"	16-lb	7.50
"	16-lb	7.25	"	18-lb	7.75
"	18-lb	7.50	"	20-lb	8.00
"	20-lb	8.00	"	24-lb.	9.60
17 x 22,	9-lb	4.50	17 x 28,	16-lb	8.00
"	10-lb	5.00	"	20-lb	8.75
"	12-lb	6.00	"	24-lb	9.50

IMPERIAL IRISH LINEN.

Price Per 500 Sheets.   Discount 20 Per Cent.

17 x 22,	11-lb	$4.00	19 x 24,	20-lb	$6.00
"	13-lb	4.50	"	24-lb	7.00
"	16-lb	5.00	"	28-lb	8.00
"	20-lb	6.00	21 x 33,	42-lb	12.00
17 x 28,	28-lb	8.00	"	52-lb	15.00
19 x 24,	16-lb	5.00			

CAXTON BOND.

Price per 1,000 Sheets. Discount 40 Per Cent.

17 x 22, No. 16 ..... $9.00	17 x 28, No. 16 ...$11.00
" " 21..... 12.00	" " 21...... 14.00
" " 25 ..... 14.00	" " 25...... 17.50
19 x 24, " 16...... 11.00	19 x 30, " 21...... 17.50
" " 21...... 13.75	22 x 28, " 21...... 21.00
" " 25...... 16.50	" " 25...... 27.00

COMMERCIAL BOND.

Price per 1,000 Sheets. Discount 20 Per Cent.

14 x 17, No. 16 ..... $5.75	19 x 24, No. 16..... $11.00
" " 18 ..... 6.25	" " 18...... 12.00
" " 21..... 7.00	" " 21...... 13.75
" " 25..... 8.75	" " 25...... 16.50
" " 29..... 10.00	" " 29...... 19.00
15 x 19, " 16 ..... 7.00	17 x 28, " 16...... 11.50
" " 18..... 8.00	" " 18...... 12.50
" " 21..... 8.75	" " 21...... 14.00
" " 25...... 10.50	" " 25...... 17.50
" " 29...... 12.00	" " 29...... 20.00
17 x 22, " 16...... 9.00	19 x 30, " 16...... 14.00
" " 18...... 10.00	" " 18...... 16.00
" " 21...... 12.00	" " 21...... 17.50
" " 25 .. .. 14.00	" " 25 ..... 21.00
" " 29...... 15.75	" " 29...... 24.00

PURE IRISH LINEN.

Price per 500 Sheets. Discount 20 Per Cent.

17 x 22, 11-lb $5.00	19 x 24, 16-lb...... $6.25
" 13-lb...... 5.50	" 20-lb. 7.25
" 16-lb...... 6.25	21 x 33, 42-lb...... 15.00
19 x 24, 13-lb...... 5.50	" 52-lb...... 18.00

CRANE'S "ALL LINEN."

Price per 500 Sheets. Discount 35 Per Cent.

17 x 28,	16-lb.........	$8.00	18 x 23,	12-lb.........	$6.00
"	20-lb.........	8.75	"	14-lb.........	7.00
"	24-lb.........	9.50	"	16-lb.........	7.25
16 x 21,	8-lb.........	4.00	"	18-lb.........	7.50
"	10-lb.........	5.00	"	20-lb.........	8.00
"	12-lb.........	5.50	"	22-lb.........	8.75
"	14-lb.........	5.75	"	36-lb.........	14.00*
"	16-lb.........	6.50	19 x 24,	14-lb.........	7.00
"	18-lb.........	7.25	"	16-lb.........	7.50
"	28-lb.........	11.00*	"	18-lb.........	7.75
17 x 22,	10-lb.........	5.00	"	20-lb.........	8.00
"	12-lb.........	6.00	"	22-lb.........	8.75
"	14-lb.........	6.25	"	24-lb.........	9.60
"	16-lb.........	6.75	"	42-lb.........	17.00*
"	18-lb.........	7.25			
"	20-lb.........	8.00			

*Ledger.

ROYAL BOND.

Price Per 1,000 Sheets. Discount 50 and 20 Per Cent.

14 x 17,	No. 16....	.$12.50	19 x 24,	No. 16......	$24.00
"	" 21......	15.00	"	" 21......	29.00
"	" 25......	18.00	"	" 25......	34.00
17 x 28,	" 16......	25.00	15 x 19,	" 16......	15.00
"	" 21......	30.00	"	" 21......	18.00
"	" 25	36.00	"	" 25.....	22.50
17 x 22,	" 16......	20.00	19 x 30,	" 16......	30.00
"	" 21......	26.00	"	" 21......	36.00
"	" 25......	30.00	"	" 25	45.00

Crane Brothers' Machine Hand-Made
"Warranted All Linen" Laid Papers.

STANDARD SIZES.			PRICE PER REAM, 500 SHEETS.
Double Cap	17 x 28,	16 lbs.	$8.00
" "	"	20 "	8.75
" "	"	24 "	9.50
Demy	16 x 21,	8 "	4.00
"	"	10 "	5.00
"	"	12 "	5.50
"	"	14 "	5.75
"	"	16 "	6.50
"	"	18 "	7.25
"	"	28 " (Ledger)	11.00
Folio Post	17 x 22,	10 "	5.00
" "	"	12 "	6.00
" "	"	14 "	6.25
" "	"	16 "	6.75
" "	"	18 "	7.25
" "	"	20 "	8.00
Medium	18 x 23,	12 "	6.00
"	"	14 "	7.00
"	"	16 "	7.25
"	"	18 "	7.50
"	"	20 "	8.00
"	"	22 "	8.75
"	"	36 " (Ledger)	14.00
Royal	19 x 24,	14 "	7.00
"	"	16 "	7.50
"	"	18 "	7.75
"	"	20 "	8.00
"	"	22 "	8.75
"	"	24 "	9.60
"	"	42 " (Ledger)	17.00

Cream or blue always in stock.   Localized Water Mark.

Discount—35 per cent. off full ream lots.
20 per cent. off broken ream lots.

Crane Brothers' Machine Hand-Made "Japanese Linen," Wove and Laid Papers.

Standard Sizes.		Price Per Ream, 480 Sheets.	
Double Cap	17 x 28,	20 lbs.	$6.00
" "	"	24 "	7.20
" "	"	28 "	7.84
Demy	16 x 21,	14 "	4.20
"	"	16 "	4.80
"	"	18 "	5.40
"	"	20 "	5.60
"	"	22 "	6.16
"	"	24 "	6.72
Folio	17 x 22,	14 "	4.20
"	"	16 "	4.80
"	"	18 "	5.40
"	"	20 "	5.60
"	"	22 "	6.16
"	"	24 "	6.72
Medium..................	18 x 23,	18 "	5.40
"	"	20 "	6.00
"	"	24 "	7.20
"	"	28 "	7.84
"	"	32 "	8.96
"	"	34 "	9.52
Royal	19 x 24,	16 "	4.80
"	"	18 "	5.40
"	"	20 "	6.00
"	"	22 "	6.60
"	"	24 "	7.20
"	"	26 "	7.28
"	"	28 "	7.84
"	"	30 "	8.40

White or blue, laid or wove, always in stock.

Discount—20 per cent. off full ream lots.
10 per cent. off broken ream lots.

CRANE AND COMPANY'S BONDS.

Price per 1,000 Sheets.

Subject to Discount of
30% off Ream Lots.
20% off Broken Lots.

SIZES.		14x17	15x19	16x21	16x24	17x22	19x23	19x24	20x24	17x28	19x30	22x28	21x33
Bond.	Thickness No. 16	$12.50	$15.00	$17.50	$20.00	$20.00	$23.00	$24.00	$25.00	$25.00	$30.00	$32.00	$36.00
"	No. 18	13.50	16.50	20.00	22.00	23.00	25.00	26.00	27.00	27.00	33.00	36.00	40.50
"	No. 21	15.00	18.00	22.50	25.00	26.00	28.00	29.00	30.00	30.00	36.00	40.00	45.00
"	No. 25	18.00	22.50	27.00	31.00	30.00	33.00	34.00	36.00	36.00	45.00	47.00	53.00
"	No. 29	20.00	24.00	29.00	32.00	32.00	36.00	38.00	40.00	40.00	48.00	52.00	58.50
"	No. 36	25.00	30.00	35.00	40.00	39.00	45.50	47.50	50.00	50.00	59.50	64.00	72.00
"	No. 43	30.00	35.50	42.00	47.50	46.50	54.50	56.50	60.00	60.00	71.00	76.50	86.00
"	No. 55	38.00	45.50	53.50	61.00	59.50	69.50	72.50	76.00	76.00	90.00	98.00	110.00
Premium Bank Note	No. 22	18.00	21.50	25.50	29.00	29.00	32.50	34.00	36.00	36.00	43.00	46.00	51.50
Parchment Deed	No. 31	28.00	34.00	40.00	44.00	44.00	50.00	53.00	56.00	56.00	68.00	73.00	82.00
" "	No. 37	34.00	40.00	47.50	53.00	53.00	60.00	63.50	67.00	67.00	81.00	87.00	98.00
" "	No. 44	40.00	47.50	56.50	62.00	62.00	71.00	75.00	81.00	81.00	96.00	103.00	116.00
Artificial Parchment	No. 56	60.00	72.00	84.00	96.00	95.00	110.00	114.00	120.00	120.00	144.00	155.00	174.00

PARSONS' BOND SAME PRICE AS ABOVE.

Less 35% Reams.
25% Broken.

4711 BOND.

Price per 1,000 Sheets. Discount 25 Per Cent.

15 x 19, No. 21......	$6.50	19 x 24, No. 21......$10.00
" " 25......	7.50	" " 25 . ... 12.50
" " 29	9.00	" " 29...... 14.00
17 x 22, " 21	8.00	19 x 30, " 21...... 13.00
" " 25......	10.00	" " 25...... 15.00
" " 29	11.50	" " 29...... 18.00
17 x 28, " 21......	10.50	22 x 34, " 21 ..... 16.00
" " 25......	12.50	" " 25 ..... 20.00
" " 29......	14.50	" " 29...... 23.00

CONGRESS BOND.

Price per 1,000 Sheets. Discount 40 Per Cent.

14 x 17, No. 16......	$5.50	19 x 24, No. 16......$11.00
" " 18	6.25	" " 18...... 12.00
" " 21......	7.00	" " 21...... 13.75
" " 25	8.75	" " 25...... 16.50
" " 29......	10.00	" " 29...... 19.00
15 x 19, " 16......	7.00	17 x 28, " 16. .... 11.00
" " 18......	8.00	" " 18...... 12.50
" " 21......	8.75	" " 21 ..... 14.00
" " 25......	10.50	" " 25 ..... 17.50
" " 29	12.00	" " 29...... 20.00
17 x 22, " 16......	9.00	19 x 30, " 16...... 14.00
" " 18......	10.00	" " 18...... 16.00
" " 21......	12.00	" " 21...... 17.50
" " 25.....	14.00	" " 25..... 21.00
" " 29......	15.75	" " 29...... 24.00

ELMWOOD BOND.

				Per 1,000 Sheets.
14 x 17,	No.	21		$ 8.50
"	"	25		10.00
15 x 19,	"	21		10.25
"	"	25		12.00
16 x 21,	"	21		12.00
"	"	25		14.25
17 x 22,	"	21		13.50
"	"	25		16.00
17 x 28,	"	21		17.00
"	"	25		20.00
19 x 24,	"	21		16.25
"	"	25		19.50
19 x 30,	"	21		20.50
"	"	25		24.00
21 x 33,	"	21		24.50
"	"	25		29.00

Finish in rough and smooth.
10 per cent. off 1,000, less net.

LEDGER PAPERS.

Brown's, Weston's, Crane's.

Size Name.	Size Inches.	Weight.	Ream.	100 Sheets.	Qr.
Crown	15 x 19	22	$6.16	$1.29	$0.31
Double Crown.....	19 x 30	44	12.32	2.56	.62
Demy.............	16 x 21	28	8.50	1.77	.43
Demy.............	16 x 21	30	9.50	1.98	.48
Medium...........	18 x 23	36	12.00	2.48	.60
Medium...........	18 x 23	38	13.00	2.69	.65
Medium...........	18 x 23	40	14.00	2.89	.70
Royal............	19 x 24	44	15.00	3.09	.75
S. Royal	20 x 28	50	20.00	4.13	1.00
Imperial	23 x 31	72	27.00	5.57	1.35
Double Demy......	21 x 32	56	17.00	3.51	.85
Double Demy......	21 x 32	60	19.00	3.92	.95
Double Demy......	16 x 42	56	17.00	3.51	.85
Double Demy......	16 x 42	60	19.00	3.92	.95
Double Medium...	23 x 36	72	24.00	4.95	1.20
Double Medium...	23 x 36	80	28.00	5.78	1.40
Double Medium...	18 x 46	72	24.00	4.95	1.20
Double Medium...	18 x 46	80	28.00	5.78	1.40
Double Royal	24 x 38	88	30.00	6.19	1.50
Double Royal Long	19 x 48	88	30.00	6.19	1.50
Elephant..........	23 x 28	65	27.00	5.75	1.35
Colombier	23 x 34	80	32.00	6.66	1.60
Atlas.............	26 x 33	100	45.00	9.50	2.25
Double Elephant...	27 x 40	125	55.00	12.50	2.75
Antiquarian.......	31 x 53	200	100.00	20.85	5.00
Emperor..........	48 x 72	600	500.00	104.00	25.00

Cap   14 x 17, 14, 16, 18, 20 ⎫
Double Cap 17 x 23. 28, 32, 36, 40 ⎬ 28c. per lb.,
Folio   17 x 22, 20, 22, 24, 28 ⎪ less discount.
Royal Folio 19 x 24, 24, 38 ⎭

Prices subject to discount of 30% full   ream lots.
    "   "   "   20% broken "   "

COLORS CARRIED IN STOCK,

Primrose, Green, Pink, Blue, Pink Bond.

"No· 40," NEW AND IMPROVED.

NATIONAL SAFETY.

Price List.

16 x 21,	500	Sheets	$12.00
17 x 22,	"	"	13.00
17 x 24,	"	"	13.50
19 x 24,	"	"	14.50
17 x 28,	"	"	15.00
18 x 26,	"	"	15.00
19 x 28,	"	"	17.00
20 x 28,	"	"	18.00
28 x 34,	"	"	30.00
26 x 36,	"	"	30.00

Other sizes at corresponding rates.
Above prices subject to discount: Ream Lots, 25 per cent. Case Lots, 33⅓ per cent.
Broken Lots, net.

GEORGE LA MONTE,
Sole Manufacturer, 87 Maiden Lane.

Price List of Bankers' Safety Paper. Regular Sizes Carried in Stock.

14 x 17,	500	sheets	$3.75
16 x 21,	"	"	5.50
17 x 22,	"	"	6.00
17 x 24,	"	"	6.50
17 x 28,	"	"	7.50
17 x 30,	"	"	8.00
18 x 23,	"	"	6.50
18 x 26,	"	"	7.50
18 x 28,	"	"	8.00
19 x 24,	"	"	7.50
19 x 28,	"	"	8.50
20 x 28,	"	"	9.00

Other sizes furnished at short notice at corresponding rates.